ANCIENT TIDES

Division 14: Berkano Vampire Collection

J.L. WEIL

Dark Magick Publishing, LLC

Soul Symmetry

BEAUTY NEVER DIES

(Teen Dystopian Romance)

Slumber

Entangled

NINE TAILS SERIES

(Teen Paranormal Romance Short Novels)

First Shift

SINGLE NOVELS

Starbound (Teen Paranormal Romance)

Casting Dreams (New Adult Paranormal Romance)

Dark Souls (Runes Series KindleWorld Novella)

Ancient Tides (New Adult Paranormal Romance)

For an updated list of my books, please visit my website:
www.jlweil.com

Join my VIP email list and I'll personally send you an email reminder as soon as my next book is out! Click here to sign up: www.jlweil.com

Ancient Tides © 2018 J.L. Weil

In a world of secrets, blood, and magic, all the lines have blurred.

On the last day of high summer, Skylar Smoake stands on the edge of Silent Bend, overlooking the raging waters below. The black sky cracks with the angry sound of thunder and flashes blue as lightning strikes. Crying out her grief into the turbulent storm, Sky rails against the evil that has threatened her division for generations—the creatures who took everything from her—the Berkano vampires.

Sky is one of the Charmed, her powers ancient, derived from Braywen the sorceress of Glenn the Gaelics. Her duty is to a secret coven vowed to protect Division Fourteen. Trust has never been easy for Sky, not in a world where magic is shunned but necessary. She finds herself drawn to a man with secrets and a hidden past she is determined to unearth.

Zavier Cross is like no man Sky has ever encountered. With silvers eyes that shine like starlight, and a smirk she finds both charming and irritation, Zavier is a distraction she can't afford.

The vampire, Lilith, has been seeking a witch. Biding her time in the tunnels under the city, she waits poised to attack. The tension between the Bitten and the Charmed could crumble Frisco Bay, and seeking revenge is all Sky can taste.

Caught in a battle for the fate of Division Fourteen, Sky must fortify her gifts and trust the one man who has the power to crush her heart...for the ancient tides have awaken.

CHAPTER 1

I glanced over my shoulder at the cloaked figure following me in the shadows. *Move your ass, Skylar. The castle is just past the gate—safety.*

The vampire stalking me wouldn't think twice about stepping foot into the perimeter of Silent Bend. Not with the slew of guards stationed at every corner. But what had I expected when I snuck out like a thief into the night? It didn't matter I had a good reason, or I had eluded my detail.

I'd been fooling myself into thinking I'd be able to make it to and from the coven meeting without being detected by the Bitten. It didn't matter there was a peace treaty between us. This bloodsucker was dying to get his dirty claws on me, but it wasn't my magical blood he wanted. It would kill him. Nope. The asswipe wanted to impregnate me—against my will, rules be damned.

I shouldn't have been surprised I was being hunted again. It was becoming a bad routine each time I snuck out to the coven gatherings, hidden deep in the heart of Frisco Bay. One day, my luck was going to run out. A single vamp I could handle, but if they brought friends, I was going to be sorry I had left Liam back at home. Except the whole point of a secret coven meeting was no one was to know, not even my assigned guard.

If my brother Colin found out, he would be angry enough to make more than one of his trained soldiers babysit me. It was troublesome trying to find creative ways to ditch Liam alone. It helped we were sleeping together, and I doused him with a bit of a sleeping potion.

Darting across the field, I used the fog that constantly covered the city to my advantage. Vampires were stealthy, their footsteps undetected by human ears, but I wasn't human. As a witch, I could sense him, and this bloodsucker had been trailing me for the last ten minutes. I was tempted to let him catch me so I could ask why the Berkano vamps were suddenly so interested in *me*.

I was afraid I knew.

The war between vampires and witches had all but come to an end in a blink of an eye. The Rift saw to that, as well as the treaty forged. Peace seemed to be in our grasp, the accord to end the fight that had raged on between us for centuries. It had been fifty years since the night of the Rift, yet with the so-called peace came new sets of problems.

The only way vampires could grow their numbers was by procreating with a witch. There were plenty of us around, but very few full-blooded witches, and even fewer with the blood of a Rift witch. I was the *only* female witch in Frisco Bay who was a direct descendant of a Rift witch. Lucky me. I wasn't sure why that mattered to them, but I was all the above. Guess that made me special.

Creeping along the worn and pathetic chained fence that bordered Silent Hill, I expanded my senses, attempting to pick up the Bitten's aura, but the world was eerily quiet, which made me very nervous.

"Where did you go, bastard?" I whispered.

The moon provided the only source of light, barely shining through the fog. I was a bit disappointed he hadn't made a move. What was the fun in just stalking me? I was totally up for some one-on-one combat with a vamp. It had become my favorite pastime since the leeches had taken the most important person in my life from me. Assholes.

Of course, me being out here, at night and alone, was stupid, considering all the things I'd lost, but I could no longer sit aside and do nothing while the vampires prepared to wage war against us, both human and witch. Those who didn't believe the attack was coming were the real fools.

Retreat. Retreat. My instincts were urging me to hurry and slip through the hole in the fence, into the safe confines of my home, but my need for revenge and justice screamed to take out the bloodsucker and send a message. My mother's death would not be in vain.

But if my instincts were wrong, and they normally weren't, there was only one lone vampire on my tail. I didn't want to become that girl in the old movies who walked right into a trap. I was smarter than that, and those Hollywood films were now a thing of the past.

I moved further along the fence, my eyes scanning the open field, prepared to be jumped at any minute. The chain-linked metal clattered as my hand accidently ran over the top of a loose link. *Smooth, Skylar. Alert the predator to your location.*

It was pitch black, and I was bone-tired. The next time I felt the need to sneak out in the middle of the night, I was going to remember to bring my dagger. How could I have been so forgetful and careless? I knew better than to leave home without a weapon. Magic wasn't always enough. This wasn't my first experience with the Berkano vampires, and it wouldn't be my last.

Whether anyone other than the coven believed me, they were up to something. Forget the treaty. The vamps couldn't be trusted. I hoped my fortune wouldn't run out tonight.

My life was anything but normal. Life in general hadn't been since the Rift and probably never would again. On a quest to cure vampirism, a spell called the Rift broke the world. It had caused a rippled effect, shifting Earth into sixteen new continents. I lived in Division Fourteen, and it fell under my family's responsibility to make sure the division didn't just survive, but thrived.

In my twenty-two years, it still amazed me the world hadn't always been so primitive. The reality was we lived in a raw place.

Netflix—gone.

Cell phones—gone.

Fast food—gone.

It was depressing. Even more disheartening was I'd never been able to experience any of those luxuries. I'd been born into this crude world.

The only electricity was in the compound known as Silent Bend. Surrounding communities farmed, forged weaponry, constructed clothing, and hunted, all to sell their wares in the market. Regardless of the simplicity of life, we'd come a long way from the days after the Rift.

Travel to another division was a suicide mission. The

constant magically charged storms made it impossible, and the only thing keeping us safe were the protective barriers set up by my family's blood. Not to mention the insurmountable mountains. We were cut off from the rest of the world.

I couldn't stay outside any longer without pushing my luck. It was time to make a break for it. When I eased myself into the hole in the wired fence, the material of my hooded shawl caught on a shard of broken metal. *Wonderful.*

With one good yank, I heard the material rip, but instead of falling forward into Silent Bend, I was tugged back through the other side of the fence.

Son of a b—

A large, cold hand seized my throat, slamming me against the fence. My eyes quickly scanned the field behind him, looking to see if he was alone. Experience taught me I stood a better chance against one, and I only had seconds to kill or be killed.

He absorbed the darkness, fangs gleaming in the measly moonlight. Vampires all had the same sapphire blue eyes with an almost iridescent quality to them. This one was no different. "Where do you think you're going, pretty thang?" Judging by the fanged smile, the vampire didn't seem to regard me as a threat.

My hands flew up to his wrists as I fought to get air into my lungs, wrapping around large biceps. Calling my magic to the surface, I sent the bloodsucker a surprise of my own.

He hissed at the zap of magic, jumping back and giving me the opening I needed. "You little bitch." He lunged toward me.

"I've been called worse." Using the muscles I worked so hard to maintain, I extended my leg in the air, hitting him squarely in the family jewels. Believe it or not, that moved worked on vampires. It was a classic maneuver I used often. Hit them where it counted.

He grunted, doubling over like a baby. I grabbed a handful of his hair and lifted my knee up, cracking him in the nose. There was a satisfying sound. My hit didn't seem to hurt him overly much, but did ruin his balance.

So I ran. If I could just get inside the fence…

I was fast, but not fast enough to outrun a Bitten. He wrenched his fingers into my hair, and with strength I couldn't even imagine, flung me backward. I went sailing, pain exploding through my body as I hit the ground hard. My legs scraped against the rough cement, tearing flesh. I ignored the pain and rolled over.

The vampire was on top of me, his fangs leering over my exposed neck as he twisted my head to the side. "I only want a taste, honey." He chuckled, and we both knew he was lying.

I tried to move my head, but it was pointless. "My blood is forbidden," I spat.

His beefy body pinned me to the ground as his lethal fangs grazed my skin. "Do you think I care? Besides…" Grubby nails traced down the front of my shawl, pushing aside the material. "It's not your blood I want to taste." He leaned his face toward mine so I could smell the metallic scent of blood. The vampire had recently fed. And not on a burger and fries. There had been more and more blood feedings as of late, regardless that most vampires could survive without blood thanks to the curse.

Fear invaded my veins. How could I let the very thing I despised touch me? It wasn't fair. I was supposed to enact my revenge. I twisted my head from side to side, but it was a waste of energy. He pressed his mouth to mine in a brutal kiss that made me want to gag. Refusing to make this easy for him,

I used my teeth and clamped down on his bottom lip until I tasted the warmth of his blood.

The vamp jerked back, his tongue darting out to lick the drops of blood pooling at his lip. "They said you were feisty. I'm glad you didn't disappoint." He put a knee between my legs, and I stretched my fingers to try to reach the rune tattooed on my thigh.

"Hands off the merchandise, asshole," said a dangerous voice.

Liam.

I sighed, the muscles in my body going lax. My potion must not have been strong enough, or I'd been gone longer than planned. I lifted my head, brushing the strands of auburn hair out of my eyes, relaxing slightly. The vampire above me stiffened, but Liam was already moving through the darkness. He leapt down from the fence, a stake in his grasp. It wasn't an easy distance to jump, but for Liam, the drop wouldn't kill him.

The vampire broke his fall.

Liam's stake found the Bitten's heart, hitting him from the back and through the ribcage. The vampire's head fell back, mouth open in a silent cry a moment before he slumped on top of me, his dead weight crushing my body.

"A little help here?" I grunted, pushing at his torso where a blue light shimmered.

Liam straddled the vampire and me. His blond hair appeared silver in starlight and fog. He took a step backward, hoisting the vile creature off me. His body had already begun to decay, and it would be only seconds more before he burst like a balloon of ash and blinding light. I sat up, sucking in a sharp breath. The air burned in my lungs.

Liam offered me a hand, tugging me to my feet. My guard

was human—a warrior—and had the sculpted cheeks and chiseled abs to prove it. I often teased him that he was too pretty to be a warden, a keeper of Division Fourteen. The dark scowl on his face said I was about to get a lecture. "What were you thinking?" Liam demanded.

I turned slowly around, an innocent grin curling my lips. "I needed some air." The lie came easy. Liam and I had history. If he had been any of the other wardens, I would have been immediately escorted to my brother.

He shook his head, not believing a word out of my mouth, but knew better than to challenge me. He worked for me, well, my overbearing brother technically, but the wardens knew upsetting me would only infuriate Colin. And no one wanted to be on the other end of my brother's wrath. "No more games. If anything had happened to you, Colin would have had my head."

Colin ran a tad on the overprotective side. Although, he had his reasons. I was a constant thorn in my brother's side, his unruly and reckless little sis.

I lived up to the hype.

Dusting off the dirt from my cape, I met Liam's serious green eyes straight on. "Then for the safety of that pretty little head of yours, you better get me inside the manor."

He grabbed me under the arm, his brows pinched. "I swear, Sky, if you weren't so beautiful, I'd wring your neck. Do you have any idea what I went through when I woke up and saw you were missing?"

I lifted on my toes, and pressed a kiss on his cheek. "Thanks for saving me."

He sighed, shoulders relaxing. "Let's never speak of this again."

"I have a charm for that," I said, slipping through the hole in the fence.

"Don't push your luck with me tonight, so help me God."

I smiled, and trekked it up the incline toward the compound. What a freaking night.

The four-story house came into view, one of the few structures that had been rebuilt since the Rift. It was more of a compound, housing many of the wardens, their families, a training facility, and it operated like a command central thanks to my brother.

Two wardens were stationed at every entrance. The fault with my brother's security was the windows, but who would be dumb enough to scale a two, three, or even four-story structure? Me. My quarters were on the third floor, but being a witch had its perks.

"Wait," I whispered, swinging an arm in front of Liam to stop him.

He arched a brow.

"We can't just go strolling through the front door. The other wardens will notify Colin of our late-hour arrival."

"I'm not going to like this, am I?"

Mister-I-never-broke-a-rule-in-my-life, except for maybe sleeping with me, Liam was a stickler for order and laws. His world was black and white, where I lived mine in giant patches of grey. "Stand still and don't make a sound." Summoning the power of my ancestries, I waved my hand over his forearm, marking him with a rune of invisibility. Then I activated the one I had tattooed on the inside of my wrist.

The frown lines on Liam's forehead deepened. "You know I hate it when you mark me with your voodoo."

"This only works if you keep your big mouth shut." And if

we didn't bump into another witch, such as Colin. Considering the time of night, I liked our odds.

Liam and I slipped passed the two wardens and into the front circular hall. He assumed we would take the stairs to my room, but I headed toward the back of the first floor, to the kitchen. It had been hours since I'd eaten, and I was starved.

Once the door swung shut behind us, I flipped my hood off my head and turned around laughing. The kitchen was blissfully empty, so I dropped the enchantment. "That was exhilarating. Didn't it get your blood flowing?"

Liam propped a hip against the counter. "Which part? Finding you missing? The vampire looking for a baby mama? Or having to sneak into the compound using forbidden magic?"

I grinned, poking him in the chest. "All the above."

He shook his head, his lips thinning. "You need to get your head checked."

Rolling my eyes, I grabbed a roll from the bread box and broke off a chunk, popping it into my mouth.

"It's time for you to get some rest, Skylar." Liam sighed. "And this time, you're going to stay there all night, even if I have to tie you to the bed."

I lifted a single brow. "Are you getting kinky on me?"

Tired lines crinkled at the corner of his eyes, making him appear older than twenty-five. "Enough with the games." He dipped, lifting me over his shoulder and taking me by surprise.

"Dammit, Liam. Put me down," I growled. My hands fisted at his back, a waterfall of auburn hair blocking my vision.

He smacked my butt. "It's been a long night, Sky. Do us both of favor, and don't make this harder than it has to be. Or we could stay in the kitchen and talk about what you were *really* doing outside the walls."

That was the last thing I wanted to do, and Liam knew it. Humiliation colored my cheeks, and I clamped my teeth shut. After tonight, he was going to be watching me like a hawk. I'd never have two minutes to myself, and sneaking out of Silent Bend was going to be twice as hard.

Shit.

CHAPTER 2

og blanketed the dark churning waters, lapping against rocks and the sandy shore. A boat rocked outside the harbor, trying to seek refuge from the storm, fighting against the waves to reach the soft glow of a lighthouse deep in the mist. The blow of a horn sounded through the night, but quickly turned into a bloodcurdling scream as the earth began to shake. Magic trembled through the vaporous haze, and the chanting of Rift witches drowned out the roar of the sea.

I bolted upright in bed, a sheen of sweat on my brow and my heart racing like a herd of wild horses. For a second, like a beat of a hummingbird's wings, I scented the sea, heard the soft voices lift in a chant as old as time, and felt the mist upon my face as the water crashed against the cliffs. Fog seeped into the open balcony door and grew, climbing up the bed like a snake.

I blinked, unable to remember if I'd left the door open before falling asleep. The room smelled of rain and vanilla, the candle long since burned out or possibly doused by a gust of air.

The fog and the howling wind reminded me of the dream that had woken me. It was one I had often since my mother's death, and one I would likely have for many, many nights to come.

The vision of before the Rift plagued me, waking or sleeping, especially on nights when I was vulnerable or upset, when my defenses were low. It was through my blood I was able to see what my mother had done, what she had been a part of so many years ago. Fifty years it had been, and there wasn't a day that went by that I didn't think of her, didn't miss her.

She had been taken from me when a young girl had needed her mother most, and for that, I would never forgive the Berkano vampires. She had been robbed of watching her little girl grow into a woman, and I had been refused the comfort of a mother's arms. I often wondered if she would approve of the woman I'd become. Raised mostly by Colin, I hadn't exactly had a typical childhood. Where other girls dressed up dolls, learned to cook, or braided each other's hair, I played with swords and daggers, and always had my nose in a spell book.

Magic existed. It was everywhere, all around us, in the vibrant colors of a rainbow after a summer storm, in the song of the sea, and the glitter of a million stars on a cloudless night. The world was filled with wonders big and small, even after the Rift.

Some said the greatest magic was love, such a simple and extraordinary part of life.

I said that was bullshit. I didn't want love. I wanted sweet, blissful revenge. And one day soon, it would be mine, and there was nothing Colin or Liam could do to stop me.

My bloodline was old. My power was ancient. And my

responsibility to the craft was demanding, a legacy handed down through the generations. The power of Glenn of the Gaelics ran in my blood, derived from Braywen the sorceress, my mother. Legends of her sorcery was still whispered from one end of the valley to the other, deep in the shadows and always in secret, for the craft must be protected.

From the time I could walk, I understood that such a gift came with a price. Magic was to be respected, or pay the cost twofold, but not everyone agreed with my mindset. Take my brother. Colin was a witch, but he never used his magic, not even in battle. He tolerated my *hobby*, but only in secret.

I had taught myself how to use my gift, honed it from the books my mother had kept hidden in her rooms. They were mine now, and I treasured them, the last bit of her that remained. It was my homage to her, learning and protecting the gift she had given me.

The fire in the hearth had flickered down to a few sparks of glowing embers, and the howling wind chased through the brightly colored room. I liked bold things. A chair sat in the corner next to the fireplace, hand-woven pillows on the seat. The floor was wood that had seen better days, worn and scraped. A pretty rug of deep burgundy peeked out from under the bed. It might not be a palace, but it had been mine since I was little.

Wrapping a blanket over my shoulders, I padded to the wide arched opening that led to the balcony. *Plop. Plip. Plop.* Drops of rain hit the glass and the side of the stone compound in a chorus of a sad song, as if it felt my pain. Thunder cracked across the sky, shaking the air. I pressed my cheek to the window, gazing into the dreary fog. It was the rain that made me think of her. The lash of it battered against the windows, drummed the rooftop, and blew its icy breath underneath the wooden doors.

I'd never lived in the world prior to the Rift, but the feel of jeans on my thighs was so vivid, as was the liveliness of San Francisco.

The hooded robe that cloaked my body wasn't silk or pretty. It was practical and boring. Not that I needed pretty things, but seeing the visions that came more frequently of late made me yearn for the world before it went to shit.

Frisco Bay. It wasn't glamorous or high tech. It survived the Rift, after the hard work and determination of those who had the will to carry on, but it still had a long way to go. And my brother was the leader people turned to. He was someone my parents would have been proud of.

A deep ache took up residency in my bones, a combination of the fight from last night and an emotional scar that had yet to heal. Humans might have found a way to live with the bloodsuckers, but I didn't trust the vampires. And if the humans were smart, neither should they.

The walls of my room had become a prison I had to break free from. The cliffs of Silent Bend were at the edge of the far back corner of the compound, where the ground dropped to the dark waters of the sea. It was there I sought sanctuary when the world was too much for me to handle. And it was there I snuck to under the disguise of magic. Liam would have to get over it.

I left my room, and slipped out of the compound, invisible to the eye. My feet glided through the fog, my red cloak dancing behind with the wind. At the peak of Silent Bend, the water raged below the cliff and lightning struck blue in the black sky. The wind shrieked like a banshee, whipping my hair, sending it into a tangle of ribbons.

On the brink of the bluff, high above the sea, I stood fearless in the eye of the storm as death flew in with the fog. I could feel its hot breath on my face. For below, in secret, an army of vampires gathered, plotted, and lurked. I couldn't explain how I knew any more than I could explain the power of magic. I just knew.

Rain swept in from the sea in a thick curtain, jagged spears of lightning hurling down from the sky. I screamed, railing against all the pain and rage that consumed me night and day, for there was also a storm within me, as dark and vicious as the one that took the Bay by surprise.

Grief. Anger. Power.

The cocktail was a dangerous potion, and it flashed in my eyes, bold and blue like the violent spears of light shooting across the sky. There was something about storms that called to my blood, the power and recklessness of nature. It could never be contained or controlled.

"My mother might have started this with her magic, but it will end with mine," I vowed.

Throat dry and burning, I turned back toward the manor. Fog blanketed everything—the houses below, the cliffs, the sea, even the overgrown thicket of woods bordering Frisco Bay. In the shadows of the storm-tossed trees, in the hiss of the violent winds, I sensed death.

After the Rift, the vampires had scattered to the caves, rebuilding their clan as we rebuilt the fallen city. Lilith, the most feared and ruthless vampire in the Bay, ruled the Bitten. The vampires' hunger for blood no longer held them sway. Older, more powerful vampires like Lilith were released from their bonds to the night. Vampires had evolved, and were searching for new methods to grow their clans.

The fog made life in the Bay difficult, but it was the

Berkano vampires who destroyed our world. They threatened the fabric of our foundation.

❦

SOAKED TO THE BONE, I dripped into the bathroom and let the heavy cloak fall in a sodden heap on the floor. We had strict water restrictions, among other things, but I didn't care. I needed to warm my body, chase the chill of the rain and the foreboding of death I was sure to come.

Under the hot spray, I washed away the stain of darkness, let the water cleanse my soul with a bit of help from the enchanted soap I made myself. It cleared the mind, refreshed the body, and renewed energy.

Finally clean and feeling half human, I met my reflection in the mirror. My eyes were aqua, a feature I'd inherited from my mother. I favored her in looks, but my temperament was all my father. He had passed a year after the vampires had taken my mother, changing my life forever.

The man who had seemed invincible had died of a broken heart. I never blamed him for giving up. It was hard living with grief, but my desire for revenge kept me going.

And Colin needed me.

The door to my room burst inward, and my brother, a fierce frown marring his normally handsome features, stormed in. We shared the same eyes, but his hair was a lighter shade than mine, lacking the red highlights. "Where have you been?" he demanded.

I sent my brother a look of annoyance. "Have you forgotten how to knock?"

His lips thinned, and the muscle in his jaw ticked in aggravation. "You didn't answer the question."

I rolled my eyes, turning my back. "Out. I needed to clear my head."

"You know you're not allowed to leave the compound without Liam," he stated, sounding like a broken record. I'd heard this statement countless times. It was tiresome.

"I went to the cliffs. I had another dream," I replied, knowing how to diffuse Colin's temper.

As predicted, his eyes softened. "Sky, you have got to let it go. You can't bring them back. How can I protect you if you constantly disobey the rules?"

"Your rules suck."

"This was the last time. Do you hear me?"

"How can I not? You're yelling." So much for diffusing the situation. Colin had a temper, but I had one to match.

He exhaled, roughly raking a hand through his light brown hair. "Sky, you need to be protected. Every day I hear more reports of vampires scouring the villages for witches. Do you know what they would do to you if they found you?"

I coughed. *Did I ever*. Best not to tell Colin how close I'd come to possibly siring a vampire baby. He'd never let me leave the compound again. "I know the dangers out there. I'm not a child to be coddled, Colin."

I could argue with him until I was purple in the face. When Colin made up his mind about something, there was nothing anyone could do or say that would change his mind. He'd inherited my father's stubbornness.

"We're changing the guards. You have two minutes to get downstairs to meet your new assignment."

"Isn't that a bit extreme? Liam has been my warden for years."

"And that's the problem. He cares too much for you, and he allows you too many liberties. I'm putting an end to it.

What personal relationship you two have is your own business, but you need a warden you can't manipulate with your body."

So much for thinking the relationship was a secret. Apparently, we hadn't been fooling anyone but ourselves, not that it mattered overly much to me. I cared for Liam, but I didn't love him. When our fling began, I knew it would have to end sooner or later. Besides, Liam had become a tad too affectionate for my liking. Although, it had never been my intention to break my brother's best friend's heart.

"As you wish, *Commander*." Colin hated when I called him that. To him, he was just my brother. Yet to me, he was more like a warden.

He sighed, and then stormed out much like how he had stampeded in, with purpose and force. That was Colin.

I walked down to the main hall where my brother stood with his wardens, the stone steps echoing under my boots. A mix of humans and witches, the wardens were men who showed physical strength, a sharp mind, and impressive combat skills, but most of all loyalty to Frisco Bay. There was a treaty with the vampires, but it needed to be enforced, and that was what the wardens did.

Liam's gaze flickered to my face when I came to stand beside Colin. I could see the muscle ticking in his jaw. Liam wasn't happy. He must know Colin had decided to remove him as my personal guard. But if I had my way, I wouldn't have a warden following me at all.

Colin went into one of his long-winded speeches. I immediately checked out until he said my name. "Liam will no longer be Skylar's warden, but will now oversee the training of the guards."

Visibly gritting his teeth, Liam nodded. "If you feel it is

best." He stepped back. No one else would have noticed, but I knew Liam well, and there was no mistaking the hurt that had flickered briefly in his green eyes. He would take being removed as my warden personally.

My heart went out to him. Liam had done nothing wrong. It was my fault he was being transferred to the training grounds. I would apologize to him later, once I figured out a way to ditch my new babysitter.

"Zavier," Colin said, summoning one of the men.

I waited with a lack of interest to see which one of the chumps my brother had chosen. In a way, I felt sorry for him. He didn't know what he was in for when it came to keeping track of me. It wasn't easy containing a witch, particularly one as powerful as I was.

My lips twitched in amusement, but the small smile died when I got my first glimpse of my newly assigned warden.

The man who stepped out of the line was tall, a few inches more so than the others, with a lean and angular face and slashing cheekbones. His eyes were as silver as starlight, deep and filled with secrets. The contrast of that black hair, those dark brows, and his wild smoky eyes added to his sex appeal. But it was his lips that captured my wandering gaze. God… those lips were perfect.

For one mad moment, I saw myself tangled with him, naked under the sheets with moonlight bathing my skin. His hungry lips devoured mine. Then his hands were in my hair, sweeping it back from my face in a gesture of urgency that left me shuddering in desire. His mouth left mine to roam over my face, to find that throbbing pulse at my throat. I arched into his lips, felt myself drowning in him.

Holy crap. Get a hold of yourself.

A hot flush stole over my cheeks, spreading to certain

points in my body. I blinked, dispelling the vision or fantasy—whatever it had been—from my head. The shadow of fate had wrapped its coils of darkness around Zavier and me, but I didn't know why. What did this warden have to do with me? Would he stand in the way of what I had vowed to do?

I'd like to see him try.

Colin put a hand on the silver-eyed warden. "Zavier Cross, this is my sister Skylar. Don't be fooled by her innocent looks. She is trouble."

Trouble.

The word echoed in my head. If anyone was going to cause trouble, it was Zavier Cross. Loads of it.

CHAPTER 3

"I think I can handle her." He winked, staring at me as if he could tell what was going on in my head.

I narrowed my eyes, crossing my arms over my chest. "We'll see. I've yet to meet a man who could."

Zavier arched a brow, and I took it as a challenge.

I raised one of my own in response.

There was something unusual about this particular warden, but I couldn't put my finger on it. And try as I might, my intuition alone wasn't enough, which meant I was going to have to use magic…later, when Colin wasn't around. He hated my method of reading someone's essence. It was a bit intimate, but how else was I to accurately read a person's true nature, if not by getting a little close?

My first impression of Zavier when I got past his ridiculously good looks was I didn't trust him. Not with my life. I had to wonder how he had gained my brother's trust to be given such a position. It wasn't an easy feat, being someone my brother depended on.

Colin's brows pinched, a common expression whenever he

was displeased with me, which was often. "Remember, Zavier, when I told you this wouldn't be an easy job? Don't underestimate her, but I trust *you* to keep her from getting into trouble."

A few of the wardens shifted or chuckled. Most of them knew me well. My brother had no idea how close he was to being turned into a flaming toad. "Am I done here?" I snapped.

Colin's golden-hued skin crinkled as his eyes narrowed. "Zavier, don't let her out of your sight. A little piece of advice —sleep with one eye open and a hand on your blade."

I wasn't sure if he was warning Zavier about me or the dangers lurking outside the compound. It didn't matter.

Liam stood rigid, his gaze straight ahead, avoiding mine. I scoffed and whipped around, leaving the hall in hurried strides with Zavier on my heels. There was nothing I could do to change my situation. I was stuck with Zavier...for now. Not saying a word, I tried to ignore the dominating force behind me. The warden had a presence about him, and it was getting to me...not in a good way.

Maybe I was butt sore about Liam no longer being my guard. Losing him meant I was going to have to work harder at gaining my freedom, because without it, I couldn't seek the revenge I sorely needed.

After I turned the corner, I spun around to face Zavier. He stopped and glanced down at me with intrigue. I was about to do something I normally would never do with someone I just met. It was a risk exposing my gift, but in this case, it was one I was willing to take. Instinct told me there was more to Zavier than met the eye.

I stretched up and sealed my lips to his, taking the warden by surprise. He didn't strike me as someone who startled easily, but he recovered quickly, becoming a willing partner.

My palms flattened on his firm chest, his muscles bunching under my fingertips. For the first time, my magic failed me. I could tell a lot about a person through a simple kiss. My power gave me the ability to taste the purity of someone's soul. Human. Witch. Vampire. Those I could usually distinguish with a glance, but in instances where it wasn't clear, a kiss could tell me so much more.

Except with Zavier Cross, apparently.

I had only meant to press our lips together in a harmless kiss. What I hadn't expected was to lose myself in the kiss. My plan completely backfired.

His lips were soft and warm, and a flutter that had no business being there moved through my belly. Never had I felt such elation before. I tilted my head to the side, drawing closer when I should have pushed him away.

When the kiss ended, I was more confused than ever.

This was bad.

Who the hell was Zavier Cross? More importantly, *what* was he?

My eyes fluttered open. For a heedless moment, I wanted to lean into him, but I relied on no man. I snapped into focus, abruptly straightening and tipping my chin.

"Do you kiss all your personal guards like that?" he asked, a mocking smile curling his lips.

And just like that, the haze from the kiss was replaced with irritation. "No, only the ones with something to hide. I was reading your essence."

"You're a witch."

I smiled. "Is that going to be a problem?"

"Only if you poison me. What did you learn from our kiss?" Amusement rippled from him.

I angled my head, nibbling on my lower lip. "Other than you're arrogant? I'm not sure yet."

His lips curved. "Do we need to try it again?" he asked, his voice husky as he dipped his head.

I flattened my hands on his chest. "In your dreams."

"Too much for you to handle?"

I snorted. "Let me guess, you're used to girls falling at your feet? I bet those brooding eyes and cocky grin get you plenty of pussy. I'm not looking for a fun time. At least, not yet."

He didn't seem fazed by my language. Was the man unshakable? "I can't help it if I'm exceptional at everything I do."

"I'll be the judge of that."

"Is Liam going to be a problem?"

I paused. "No, why would he?"

He shrugged. "The rumors are he is more than your shadow."

Ugh. The gossip mongrels were even present after a world-altering event. Weren't there better things to do than worry about what I was doing behind closed doors? "Liam knows I do what is best for the division. He is needed to train the incoming guards. The future of the Bay depends on everyone keeping the treaty in place."

"So, you're an item?" he pushed.

I raised a brow. "Why the sudden interest in my love life? One kiss and you're suddenly staking claim?"

"I don't want to feel the backlash for removing him from his station. After all, he is my superior."

"You can thank my overbearing brother for that. There's no need to worry about Liam. He isn't the jealous type."

My new warden made an hmphing sound in the back of his throat.

I didn't have time for this. There were things I must do, and arguing with Zavier wasn't one of them. "Let's get one thing straight. My personal life is none of your fucking business. What I do, who I see, and who I let into my bed at night doesn't concern you."

"Your brother made it clear that everything about you concerns me," he retorted in a lazy way I found irksome.

I stepped into his personal space, tipping my chin to meet his eyes. "It would be best if you don't forget what I am."

His eyes swept the length of me. "After that introduction, there is no way I could possibly forget."

I let out a growl of aggravation and continued walking down the corridor, knowing he would shadow my every move. *Wonderful.* "And stop staring at my ass," I tossed over my shoulder.

He only chuckled.

⚜

AFTER THE RIFT, those who remained tried to pick up the pieces and put some semblance of normalcy back into the division. My parents had been part of the original group to rebuild, and part of the vision had been the creation of jobs to sustain life. Everyone did his or her part. Colin took care of law and order. My friend Tulip's mother was into herbs and plants. Other people had jobs that matched their skills.

I spent my days at my little shop in the market. My evenings were for magic. But I was able to incorporate elements of my gift into the shop. The long days in Frisco Bay could be gruesome on the body. I offered relief in a way that didn't freak out the humans. Soaps, oils, shampoos, lotions, candles, and other remedies that were made with love and a pinch of magic. What they didn't know couldn't hurt them. And besides, I was helping. My handmade products were known throughout the Bay.

The demand kept me busy. So much so that I had asked Tulip to become my partner. It was more than hiring my best friend. It was smart business. I got most of my herbs from her mother, so when I needed to replenish my stock, Tulip could grab them.

The work was gratifying, and I enjoyed the bustle of the market. It was the only time during the day I didn't feel trapped. The shop—Nature's Elixir—was truly mine, something I'd built from the ground up, and being here relaxed me. I adored the ambience, a reflection of who I was under the rage and sorrow.

Cheerful white blossoms curled like garland around an iron trellis outside the window, and when the wind blew in from the north, it carried the scent of the sea with the perfume of wisteria. There were little knickknacks and wooden carved figures customers often traded when coin was tight, as it was most days. Above the door was a starry wind chime that tinkled when someone came in.

As it did now. It wasn't a customer, though, just Tulip moseying in for the day. My partner didn't have the same drive or determination I did, but she had a way with people, an aura that drew them in.

Curling waves spilled over her milky white shoulders in the reds and golds of autumn. Her sapphire dress sashayed with her movements as a bangle of silver bracelets winked brightly on each wrist. "Whatcha cooking? Smells lovely, like lavender and vanilla."

Tulip had a nose for herbs. "It is. An oil to quiet the busy mind—a sleep tonic."

She dropped into the seat beside me. "You are definitely going to have to give me a sample for tonight. I don't think I can take another sleepless night."

"You might want to try sleeping alone for once."

Her cupid-bow lips curved up. "What fun is that?"

Tulip changed guys like I changed my bra. Daily. No judgment from me. She was her own woman, and if sampling a variety of men like they were a brunch buffet made her happy, more power to her. "Who was the lucky stud last night?" I stirred the batch of lavender and vanilla soaking in a gleaming copper pot.

"Toren." She tapped a finger to her bottom lip, leaning against the wall with a dreamy expression in her violet eyes.

Toren was one of the wardens who worked for my brother. "Oh, Tulip, do be careful. That one has a gentle heart. He will fall in love with you in a minute, if he hasn't already."

"Yes. I noticed, and it did have me a bit worried, but he was too cute to resist." She made a breathy gasping sound. Something, or someone, had caught her eye. "Who's the new tall, handsome stranger darkening your doorway?"

I stretched my legs, working out the stiffness of sitting in the same spot for too long. "My new warden."

"Don't tell me. Mr. Stick-in-the-mud found about your moonlight circle meetings."

"No, at least I don't think he did. He claimed Liam was too lenient with me, because we were sleeping together."

She snorted. "Men." Her eyes returned to Zavier. He stood at the entrance of the shop, guarding the only way in or out. Tulip's leg bounced as she bit the side of her lip. "Maybe I should properly introduce myself."

"Not necessary." For some unexplained reason, I didn't want Tulip fawning all over Zavier.

She flipped her vibrant red hair. "What the frick, Sky? Don't tell me you're sleeping with him, too."

I rolled my eyes. "I'm not sleeping with Zavier."

"Zavier…" She rolled his name off her tongue as if she were savoring it. "God, even his name is dreamy."

I frowned. "He's a pain in my ass."

She leaned back in her chair, eyes roaming over the warden. "And what a fine ass indeed. I don't see the problem. Why aren't you sleeping with him?"

Of course Tulip wouldn't see a problem with sleeping with two different guys. From the time we were five, she'd been boy crazy. It was a miracle we were ever friends since we were such opposites. "He hasn't even been my guard for twenty-four hours."

"And?"

"He isn't Liam."

She pulled pretty violet eyes from Zavier, looking at me with a serious expression, one she didn't wear often. "I thought you broke things off with Liam."

"I did. I mean, I will." I'd been trying to end things for weeks.

"You haven't told him? Sky, what are you waiting for? The longer you drag this out, the harder it is going to be. You know he has already developed feelings for you. Why string him along?"

She was right. I knew it. And I'd had every intention of telling Liam I didn't think it was a good idea for us to be involved anymore, but the whole thing with the vampire happened, and then he was reassigned. A part of me had hoped whatever there was between us would sort of die off. I was being a wuss. The last thing I wanted to do was hurt

Liam, and I didn't want anything to destroy our friendship. I cared for him, just not the same way he did for me.

I was foolish to let things progress with him. It had been stupid of me to get involved to begin with, but I had been alone and vulnerable after my father had passed. Liam had been there for me as long as I could remember, and one thing led to another, but too much time had passed, and I couldn't continue to lean on him as I had. He deserved someone so much better. I didn't have it in my heart to love someone, not when I was consumed with so much hate and vengeance.

"You're right. I will pull up my goddamn big-girl panties and talk to him."

"Good. Now let's get back to that tall drink of water. How can you even get any work done when he's around?" Tulip grinned.

I laughed. It was like her to take my mind off everything, but it was only a temporary fix, because by the end of the day, I was reminded of what had been taken from me, and what I must do.

CHAPTER 4

I opened the doors to the terrace, letting in the night and the moon, the scent of the sea and the cool crisp breeze. A shiver danced over my skin. I was avoiding sleep as I did most nights.

The dreams of the past wouldn't relent, no matter how much I pitted my will against them. Nowadays, the only way I slept without the dreams of blood and battle was with a potion. The normal aids of crystals no longer worked. It was as if the dreams were trying to send me a forewarning—something wicked was coming our way.

Damn if I didn't feel it in my bones, but my brother wouldn't listen. Hardheaded he was, and it was utterly foolish of him to think the measly truce we had between the witches, vampires, and humans would last forever. There would come a day when we would walk the path of death and pain.

In the distance, the sea tumbled, the storm from this morning had since past, but in the whistle of the wind, I heard my name.

Skylar Smoake.

And with it came the weeping of a woman. She cried for the future, for her children, and for the war that was on the horizon—the sobs of a witch who never got the chance to right a wrong.

Rubbing my hands up and down my arms, I tried to chase away the chill that had settled within me. The Bay was on the edge of something big, and as I glanced over the foggy tree-tops and the misty waters, seeing the wreckage left behind from the curse, I wondered if the world would ever be a safe place again.

On a sigh, I stepped inside and got a jolt seeing Zavier standing in the corner of the room, watching me with those intense eyes. My mind went blank for a moment, as it seemed to when I saw him unexpectedly. I couldn't look away.

"Were you spying on me?" I asked, a tad sharply. I didn't like the way the sight of him messed with my head or made me so edgy.

His smirk boosted up several degrees. "It's kind of my job."

If he kept looking at me like that, I was going to shove my foot up his ass. "And you take your job seriously, don't you?"

One dark brow arched. "Is this you trying to read me again?"

My lips pursed. This wasn't going to work. Not. At. All. He was supposed to make me feel safe, not like I wanted to pull my hair out...or worse...kiss him again. His gaze had a hypnotic effect, and if I weren't a witch, I would have thought he cast a spell over me. "Why? Do you have something to hide?"

"No more than you."

My gaze narrowed. Was he implying I had secrets—that he knew about my late-night rendezvouses? Had Liam told him?

He wouldn't do that to me. I couldn't believe Liam would rat me out like that, even if he was trying to protect me. But there was no doubting the glint of mischief in Zavier's silver eyes. *Play it cool, Sky. Don't let him get under your skin.* "I don't have secrets."

He pushed off the wall, and swaggered over to stand in front of me. "Lies don't become you, minx."

My chin went up. "I have a name. And in case you've forgotten, it's not minx."

"There are a hundred names I could call you. Proud, fierce, gorgeous, strong, powerful, *minx*," he rattled off. "But a liar wouldn't have been one of them."

I hated that he made me feel guilty. What he said was true. I wasn't a liar, not normally, not to people I loved. Deceitful when it was necessary, but a bald-faced liar wasn't part of my character. Yet, lately, it seemed the lies came too easily to my tongue. And it hadn't escaped my ego that he thought I was gorgeous. "What makes you think I'm lying?"

A keen light reflected in his eyes. "Call it a sick sense. If you are intuitive enough, you can taste a person's emotions… and yours just went from a sad tasteless blueberry to a sour green apple."

I rolled my eyes. "My emotions are not fruits."

His lips quipped. "You were in deep thought when I came in. Why the long face? And remember, I'll know if you're lying."

I frowned as I eyed him. *Crap*. He saw too much, and it was unnerving. I was going to need to find a way to hide my emotions around him. "How was your first day as my warden? Exciting, I bet." Yeah, I completely ignored his attempt to get me to open up. I wasn't in a sharing mood.

Zavier wandered to the opening of the terrace, dark,

intense eyes scanning the sky. His lips twitched. "No one tried to kill you, so I'd say it was pretty tame."

"Give me a few more days," I mumbled. "There's bound to be an attempt on my life." His midnight hair tumbled around the sharp angles of his face. He was handsome. There was no denying that. "Do you have family here in Frisco Bay?" I asked, curious to know more about the man who was such a quandary to me.

Amusement crept across his striking features. "Is this you trying to get to know me? Or you not wanting to talk about yourself?"

"Both." I smiled. "See, I didn't lie." I found riling him to be delightfully satisfying.

"My mother and brother live in the Bay."

"And is your brother also part of the guard?"

He chuckled low in his chest. "No. He chose a different path."

I laid a hand on the fireplace mantel, the corner of my lips tipping. "Hmm, sounds familiar."

"I assume you are talking about you and Colin."

"In this case, you assume right. We couldn't be more opposite. Colin believes I should be thinking about getting married, settling down, and all the other things good girls do."

"But you're not a good girl?" he drawled.

I snorted, giving him a dry stare. "What do you think?"

He turned his body toward me, leaning a shoulder against the doorframe so the moonlight spilled onto the side of his face. "I think you're complex. You've had a lot to deal with at a young age, and you've been carrying the pain with you ever since."

"You don't give up." I found the quality both annoying and

respectable. "Maybe you should have been a shrink or something."

He closed the distance between us with little effort. "I'm a physical guy." Something flared in his eyes, brightening them. "What are all these markings on your body?" His finger traced the one on my arm, sending tendrils of tingles over my skin.

I wished he would stop touching me. "You can see the runes?" I asked, suspicion and surprise clouding my voice. They were symbols used for protection, defense, healing, and any spell a witch with a grudge might need in a moment's notice.

"Is that what they are, more voodoo?" Doubt crossed his features.

"Do you have something against magic?" If he was *just* human, he shouldn't have been able to see the runes on my skin. Zavier was something more, but what?

Vampire?

If that were true, then why didn't I sense it? Vampires could see the runes I etched into my body. Something in their eyes allowed them to detect a witch's magic. Unfair? Definitely. But then again, my blood was poisonous to the leeches. He didn't have the eyes of a vampire either. All vampires in the Bay had the same cobalt iridescent color.

He shrugged. "I don't trust it."

A feeling of unease wormed its way into my belly. "I guess that makes us even, considering that is exactly how I feel about you."

A smug grin remained on his lips. "What does this one mean?"

I frowned. If he could see my runes, then using magic on him wasn't going to be as easy as it had been on Liam. Zavier had resistance to charms, which might explain why I hadn't been able to read his essence. "That I am going to kick your ass if you keep touching me." I refused to move, refused to let him intimidate me.

He leaned forward, bringing our faces closer. "Your lips are saying one thing, but your body is saying something else entirely."

I could feel the heat from his chest, and it was making me think crazy thoughts. "Great. Now I can add pervert and stalker to your growing list of undesirable personality traits."

The expression on his face said he wanted to call me out on my bullshit. "Whatever floats your boat, minx."

My eyes fixed on his lips, my mind wandering to the kiss. "Do you know anything about personal space?"

"The way I see it, Liam gave you too much space." His eyes turned luminous, or maybe it was the moonlight.

"You would see it that way," I grumbled, forcing my gaze off his mouth. I glanced out the window as a cool breeze blew over my skin, and my thoughts turned to the other night when the vampire attacked me. There could be a vampire out there right now, doing God knows what. Attacking another witch like me, killing another little girl's mother. The increased number of assaults on females sent my inner alarm bells ringing, and what was I doing? I was tucked inside the compound, wondering if Zavier's lips did taste as incredible as I remembered.

He must have noticed the far-off look that suddenly sprang into my eyes. "You want to know why your brother assigned me to you. Why he trusts me."

"Duh." The question had been on my mind all day.

One side of his mouth curved up as he pulled back. "You're not the only one with abilities."

I crossed my arms over my chest. This conversation was getting interesting. "And what is it you think you can do?"

"Oh, I'm multi-talented, but one of my specialties is human emotions. And *you* have more anger surrounding you than I've ever sensed. It makes the air circling you spicy and hot, like cinnamon candies."

At least he had that right. "How are you able to sense emotions exactly? I thought only vampires had that ability? Are you telling me you're a vamp?"

"Do you always jump to so many conclusions?"

I poked him in the chest with my middle finger. "And you're avoiding the question, buddy." He didn't budge, and I angled my head to the side. "For some reason, I can't figure out what you are, but I don't give up so easily. Sooner or later, I will find out."

"Why do I have to be put into a box or labeled? I read feelings. Sometimes, they speak loudly. Others are a whisper. It is the intense emotions like yours that push through whether I want them to or not."

"You can block it?"

"Most of the time, but not with you. Why do you think that is?" he asked, running a hand through his hair.

"How am I supposed to know? You're the one with the gift. I just turn assholes into snakes and rats."

"There's a lot more to you than that. You have power, real power, Skylar, yet you keep it hidden away."

"Or risk being burned at the stake."

"This isn't the Salem Witch Trials. You can come out of the closet."

He was mocking me. "What rock have you been living under? The world might know about vampires and witches, but they are far from accepting us. And vice versa. Do you think the vampires like being regulated or told what to do, by humans nonetheless?"

"Do *you* like hiding who you are?" he challenged.

He had a point, but damn if I was going to admit that to him. Nothing stayed hidden forever. Of course, I didn't like pretending I was only human. Those closest to me knew the truth, and a select few other witches in Frisco Bay. My family kept their bloodline a secret not out of shame, but caution. There weren't as many as there used to be. Vampires might not be able to drink our blood, but that didn't stop them from killing us.

Being attacked wasn't the only reason I was assigned a warden. The vampire's numbers had also been dwindling. Failed attempts at conceiving within their kind had pushed them to seek the company of witches—often without consent. They were becoming desperate, which put a big red target on my back. "No more than I like lying, but sometimes both are necessary to protect those you love," I answered.

"Do me a favor? Don't do anything stupid tonight. I'd rather not go chasing after you. It's been a helluva day."

That we could agree on. I nodded, acutely aware of him. He filled my space with a powerful male presence.

Satisfied I would stay put for the night, he crossed the room and disappeared behind the conjoining door.

Zavier Cross had something to hide.

And I was the witch to figure it out.

Exhausted, I finally gave in and curled up on the chair in the corner, letting the dreams take me, and with them came the dark, the blood thirst, and the horror.

I tossed in my sleep, but the dreams of she who was darkness plagued on. Her desire to get back what was stolen from her—from all vampires—consumed her. She would corrupt, she would kill, and she would destroy us all to get it back.

CHAPTER 5

I t was no surprise I awoke tired with a massive headache thumping at my temples. The stiff neck was an annoyance I could do without, my punishment for falling asleep sitting up in the chair. I pressed my fingers to my heavy eyes, noticing the knitted throw tucked over me that hadn't been there when I sat to rest for a few moments. My shadow was nowhere in sight, but that didn't mean he was far. The room beside me was conjoined to mine by a door, and was the quarters assigned to my warden. My guess was the man slept as light as a feather, waking and ready for a fight at the slightest sound.

There was another coven meeting in three days, and I had yet to figure out how I was going to get there. Zavier didn't strike me as someone who fell for the usual tricks that worked with Liam. It had helped tremendously I'd known Liam was a hundred percent human, but Zavier...

My intuition told me he wasn't human, witch, or vamp, and the not knowing made me nervous. I relied on my gifts far too often. It wasn't like them to fail me.

I didn't understand how my path had gotten so skewed in twenty-four hours, but I needed to find a way to get back on the right track—to get back to hunting the vampire responsible for my mother's death. Whatever Lilith had concocting down in the caves, I was going to put a stop to it.

I rose quickly, formulating a plan as I went about my morning routine. *Just another day, Sky...*or so let him think.

Grabbing a quick breakfast before there was nothing left, I was always conscious Zavier wasn't far away. For what I had planned, I needed privacy and space. The coven meeting was only three days away, and I had to discover what kind of magic worked on the elusive warden.

So began the series of tests.

The outcome was to see what Zavier could or couldn't detect. How else was I going to get to the meeting if I couldn't figure out a way to ditch my shadow?

The only other alternative was to bring him with, but I hadn't even trusted Liam with my whereabouts on those occasional late evenings. Why would I trust Zavier? I couldn't. He had already proved himself to be mysterious, and I couldn't take the chance he would expose the coven...or worse, tell my brother.

"Why are we traipsing around in the weeds?" Zavier asked as we tromped through what could have been mistaken for a jungle.

Just outside the compound gate, near the base of the cliffs, was where the thick and overgrown brush and thistle began. Eventually, if one went deep enough, it gave way to woods so dense it would be easy for someone to get lost and never be found.

The key was to never lose sight of the sea. If I couldn't hear the slushing of waves, I was too far from home.

"They aren't weeds," I told him, crouching to inspect a bushel of rosemary. "I need to replenish my stock of herbs. The things I can get myself, I'd rather not pay for."

"Makes sense. I'm wondering why *we're* doing it?"

I rolled my eyes. "Were you hit on the head when you were small?"

His mouth set into a grim line. "Uh, not that I know of."

"Beyond popular belief, I actually like getting my hands dirty occasionally."

He leveled a mischievous glance on me. "You don't say?"

I scowled. "Don't be a perv."

His grin spread, turning downright wicked. "That's like asking me not to breathe."

There was a quality about Zavier I found amusing, even when I didn't want to be charmed by him. Like now. I cut the springs of rosemary and added them to my bag.

"Since you've dragged my ass out into the wilderness, what are we looking for?" he asked.

I side-eyed him, surprised he wanted to help. Liam only ever complained and whined about being in the woods. He wasn't the outdoorsy type. I held up a sprig of rosemary. "This is rosemary. It look like short pine trees with fat trunks and long, thin branches that grow straight up. If you're unsure, smell the leaves. Rosemary has a woodsy aroma of lemon and pine."

"Where did you learn all of this?" he asked after I'd risen. We continued to walk down an off-beaten path.

I shrugged, lifting the straps of my canvas bag onto my shoulder. "Some of it I learned from spell books."

He made a chortling sound in the back of his throat.

"Hey, you asked. I'm giving you an honest answer," I replied.

"That you did," he said, reminding me he was an emotional lie detector.

"I also spent a lot of time roaming these woods with Tulip and her mom. She taught me the common plants, where to find them, and how to use them. The spell books showed me how to amplify their properties."

"The secret ingredients that makes your shop a hot spot." His eyes scanned over the surface of the forest floor, looking for bushels of rosemary. It was kind of cute, and I almost felt guilty for what I was about to do.

Almost.

But not enough to waste an opportunity.

This would be a good time to test how susceptible he was to magic. Keep him talking and busy looking for plants, and before he knew it, he'd be under my spell. I couldn't have planned it better. I touched the rune at my neck, but right before I activated the charm, Zavier grabbed my wrist.

He blinked under those ridiculously long eyelashes. "Don't even think about it, minx. None of your witchcraft."

"How did you—?" I shook my head. "What other kinds of abilities do you have? It seems you're holding out on me." No human could move that fast.

"The bigger question is, why were you going to use one of those runes?" he challenged. "Maybe I'm not the only one with secrets to hide."

"Argh," I grumbled. At least he admitted he was hiding something from me. "You're so frustrating. How can you expect me to answer your questions, when you skate right over mine?"

He still had my wrists in his grasp. He gave a quick jerk, pulling me closer to him. "Because it is my job to keep you

43

safe, even if that means pissing you off or upsetting you. I'd rather have you mad at me than hurt…or worse."

Great for him, but that wasn't going to help me. I sent a stream of electricity to my fingertips and zapped him, expecting him to release me. But that didn't happen.

I tried not to be impressed.

His fingers tightened for a moment and then relaxed. He had felt the shock. "Damn it, Skylar." Those bright silver eyes were moving quickly into no-longer-amused land.

"Can you blame a girl for trying?" I asked, pasting on my sweet and innocent smile. It worked ninety-nine percent of the time. Something told me Zavier was the one percent who would see right through my act.

I jerked back, not expecting him to release his hold on me. Imagine my surprise when I stumbled backward. Things only went downhill from there.

Literally.

I shrieked as I lost my footing, the ground falling out from underneath me. The Bay was known for its sinkholes. As I slid down the side of the muddy slope, Zavier yelled my name. I thought he was going to jump down after me, which would have been utterly stupid. I needed him to save me, not get us both killed.

It was a bumpy ride, packed with rocks scraping down my back and mud slipping into places it had no business in. The impact sent me hurtling toward the ground, and the taste of dirt made me wince.

It sucked.

My head was throbbing where I'd slammed it once or twice into the ground on my way down, not a pleasant trip. Spots danced behind my eyes. I flinched, lying still as I took a quick inventory of the aches in my body. Nothing broken, but I would for sure have some cuts and bruises.

Shoving my hands into the mud, I pushed to my feet, awareness returning hastily. Holy shit. The ground was sucking me down. *Quicksand!* The more I struggled, the tighter the pressure cradled around me.

Stay calm. No need to panic. Yet.

I stilled my movements. Zavier had been right behind me before I decided to use the side of the hill as a slip-n-slide. Any second he was going to lend me a hand. It wasn't like he was going to leave me to sink to my death.

My eyes darted left and right, searching for the warden who had been stuck by my side for the last few days. *Where the hell was he?* Just fucking great. The one time I needed his help and he was nowhere in sight. Now he suddenly decided to give me some space. What an ass.

"Zavier!" I yelled. "A little help?"

There had to be an explanation for his absence, but a solid reason was eluding me. It could also be because I was in a bit of a bind. My brain waves were jumbled, but the longer I stood there doing nothing, the more trouble I was in.

The mud was up to my calves. I knew from experience that struggling in quicksand only made things ten times worse.

Keep it together.

Easier said than done.

Almost near a full-blown freak out, I stretched my arms, grabbing onto a nearby shrub. The green foliage couldn't hold my weight, breaking off in my hand as I tugged. "Shit."

I struggled to stay motionless, giving myself time to figure out how I was going to get out of this mess. No spells came to mind.

And then I caught a blur of colors. It dashed past me, but as

I twisted around, nothing was there. "Zavier?" I called, but I wasn't shocked when no one responded.

Oh my God. I'm going to die. My brother's constant warnings about the dangers of the woods rang through my head. What would he do without me? I was the only family he had left.

The strong hand came out of nowhere, clasping onto mine. I opened my eyes, and sighed. Zavier's face came into focus. "What the hell to you so long, you jerk?" I squealed.

Muscles in his arms bunched. "You might want to save the insults until after I manage to get you out of there."

"Hurry."

Within seconds, I was wrangled from the mud trap, and pressed against him. The speed and strength in which he had managed to set me free was impressive. No human could have accomplished such a feat, but it was becoming painfully clear Zavier wasn't human.

The warmth of his body was soon replaced by a feeling of loss as he set me on my feet and moved away. His hands came to frame my face on either side of my cheeks. "You okay?" His eyes roamed over me from head to toe.

"I could have died!" I sounded ungrateful, but it had been a rough day.

"But you didn't," he replied blithely.

My eyes narrowed. "Was that your plan? To scare the shit out of me? What kind of person are you?"

Zavier grinned. "Today, I'm your knight in shining armor."

My heart fluttered a few times. Stupid heart. "I don't need a knight in shining armor."

"Everyone needs help sometimes."

"I need your help like I need a third boob."

His lips twitched. "Is that your normal reaction when someone saves your life?"

I brushed the dirt and crud from my clothes. It was a helpless cause, and I gave up with a sigh. "No. I'm used to being attacked by neckbiters, not being sucked by the earth into a deadly abyss. I don't mean to sound ungrateful; it's just I can't figure you out."

He locked me in a stare that made me forget to breathe. Damn those starlit eyes. His hand lifted, reaching toward my cheek to rub off a smear of mud. "Not everything in life is black and white. Besides, who doesn't love a little mystery?"

"I'd love to string you up by your balls, but we don't always get what we want," I mumbled, brushing off as much of the muck from my legs as possible.

His eyes flashed. "I do."

Oh, he was arrogant, all right. "You got some gonads on you."

"Thank you. They're quite exceptional, I assure you."

Keeping a straight face was becoming difficult. "I'm trying hard to ignore your egotistical charm."

He rocked back on his heels. "It's hard, isn't it? I'm like walking heroin. Very habit forming."

My lips twitched into a curl. *What the hell am I going to do about Zavier Cross?* What I wasn't going to do was give up. I would find a way to get to the coven meeting even if I had to tie Zavier up.

CHAPTER 6

I t was safe to say so far, my attempts at figuring Zavier out had failed in a big way. And the coven gathering was only two days away. While I was still weary of Zavier, I wasn't about to admit defeat. The man had to have a magical kryptonite.

And *I* would find it.

Might take me longer than I liked, but I refused to believe I had met my match. It would be a cold day in hell before that ever happened.

The moon sparkled over the blue water like glittering diamonds. I stood on the veranda at the rear of Silent Bend, looking out over the cliffs. After a much-needed shower, I'd managed to sneak up to my room without being spotted by Colin or Liam. The questions of my muddy attire would have been a hot topic and put Zavier on the spot.

Not sure why I cared whether he got chewed out, but for some unexplained reason, I didn't want Zavier to pay for what I'd been responsible for. None of today would have happened if I hadn't been determined to try my charms on Zavier as an experiment.

I knew how to take responsibility for my actions, and wasn't stupid enough to blame the events of today on anyone other than myself, regardless that Zavier could be an asshat.

Lost in thought, I didn't hear Liam sneak up on me until his arms wrapped around my waist and he whispered in my ear. "Hey, doll."

Shit.

I closed my eyes for a second, thinking how this unforeseen situation was going to pan out.

No matter how I shuffled the cards, it was going to end with someone getting hurt. There were too many other things going on in my life. I needed to end things with Liam. Tonight.

And I was dreading it like a trip to the dungeons.

Slowly, I turned in his embrace as my eyes drifted over the shadow in the corner. I swore Zavier arched a brow in my direction. "Hey. What happened to no PDA?" I asked, wiggling backward to put a little space between us.

"There is no one here," he said, trying to regain the distance, obviously disregarding Zavier. "Things have changed. I'm no longer your warden, so there's no reason to hide our relationship."

Oh, boy. This was going to be harder than I thought. *You can do this, Sky. Just like ripping off a bandage, quick and painful.* It was the best way, but the words stalled in my esophagus. "About that," I finally forced out.

"What's wrong? Don't tell me you snuck off again."

A movement from the corner caught my eye. Zavier's body had gone tight, eyes glowing in the dark. Had he heard Liam? We were far enough away it would have been difficult for a human, even if the wind had carried our voices.

I pulled my gaze from the shadows and looked at Liam. "No, it's nothing like that."

He brushed aside a lock of my hair. "Okay, then tell me what has put that troubled glimmer in your eyes. Or is it a who?"

"If you're asking about Zavier, he is fine."

"Good, if there is nothing wrong…" He regained the space between us and dipped his head, claiming my lips in a kiss.

I didn't pull away. What could one kiss hurt? And it would also be a good test to make sure I hadn't lost my touch. Maybe it wasn't Zavier, but that my abilities were off. Anything was possible, and it was better to eliminate all options.

There was a little guilt demon on my shoulder scolding me for using Liam, particularly when I was about to break up with the guy. It didn't stop me from kissing him, but it did have me ending the kiss the second I got my answer.

At the first taste of his lips, Liam's essence entered my body. All the things I had admired about the warden filtered into me, including a few dark traits, a smorgasbord of warmth and goodness, and a smidge of coldness that had an icy bite.

Liam was undoubtedly human. There was no question or confusion about it.

He had always been a pleasant kisser, and I tried to convince myself it was as equally potent as the heady-lose-my-mind kiss I'd experienced with Zavier.

Liar.

I didn't want to admit I had felt something with Zavier, something a whole lot more than what was been between Liam and me. But it only made what I was about to do justifiable. I didn't love Liam, not the way I should.

I pressed my palms to his chest. He was still wearing his warden uniform. "Liam." My eyes darted over his shoulder.

Two orbs of silver burned brightly in the night like the center of an artic storm, churning with emotion I thought might be anger.

"Why do you seem so...different tonight?"

I flashed my gaze back to Liam's almost too-handsome face, and my stomach dropped. "We need to talk."

"I'd rather do this instead," he murmured, running his lips along the spot under my ear.

I put pressure on his chest, letting him know the further advances had to stop. "This is kind of important. It's been on my mind lately."

He framed my face with his hands, and smiled a charming, boyish grin. "I haven't seen you in two days. I'm sorry if I'm distracted. You smell so good."

"You're making this hard." I groaned. "You know I care about you. You're family to Colin and me."

The fingers outlining my cheeks fell slightly, and Liam's eyes lost some of their glimmer of amusement. "Now you're making me nervous. What's going on? Did something happen?"

I swallowed. "You knew when this thing between us started that I wasn't looking for anything serious. You've been a great friend to me, and I don't know how I would have gotten through any of it without you."

His hands dropped away from my face. "Right. We were having fun. No strings attached."

"The fun's over." The words popped out of my mouth before I thought about how clipped they sounded. I winced, seeing the confusion cross over his expression. And then the hurt. Could I take back the last twenty seconds of my life? If I knew the spell, I might have used it.

And like a light had been switched, anger flipped into his

blue eyes, turning them into flames of fire. "Is this because of him?" He glared at the corner where Zavier stood.

At the sound of Liam's suddenly raised voice, Zavier shoulders stiffened, and he pushed off the wall. I needed to get this situation under control, before there was a warden-on-warden brawl on the terrace. I put my hand on Liam's shoulder. "Of course not. I've only known Zavier a few days. This has nothing to do with him, and everything to do with me." This was the right thing, wasn't I? Staring into Liam's face, I wasn't so sure anymore, but I did know it would be cruel to continue to string him along knowing my feelings for him were only lukewarm.

"Then I don't understand. I'm not asking you to be my wife right now. What's changed?" he asked, forking his fingers through his golden hair.

"Nothing. Everything." I leaned against the wooden railing, the wind picking up pieces of my tousled curls. "Liam, you know I will never be the woman you want…or need. You might be content now, but eventually you will want more, and you *should* want more. I can't give you what you deserve. I wouldn't be happy; maybe I won't ever be. But one of us should, don't you think?"

"That's not true. I know you're still hurting inside from all you've been through, but I truly believe that if you let yourself, you could be happy with me."

Maybe he was right. Maybe I could, but until the vampire who killed my mother paid the price with her life, rules be damned, I couldn't think about anything else. "Liam, if you truly knew me, you would know I can't think about marriage or love. Not right now. Someday I might want a family, but that someday isn't tomorrow. It might not even be ten years from now. I have a promise to keep."

Liam knew all about my vow to kill the vampire bitch. Didn't mean he agreed, but he knew better than to stand in my way. I was a witch after all. "I would wait for you, if that's what it takes."

"The thing is that I don't want you to wait." *Ouch*. That came out harsher than I intended.

More hurt sliced across Liam's features.

Dammit. I was bungling this entire thing. I didn't want my friendship with Liam to end, and I certainly didn't want it to get in the way of his friendship with Colin. "I'm sorry, Liam. I truly am. Things in my life are complicated right now."

"They're always complicated with you."

"I don't want you to get caught up in my problems. It will only put you in a difficult position with Colin."

His eyes narrowed. "What are you up to? If you're in danger, I can help." Just like Liam to want to stroll in and save the day. He had a bit of a knight-in-shining-armor complex.

"It doesn't matter." I refused to let him put his life in jeopardy.

"You need to let go of this ridiculous notion of revenge, Sky. If you don't, I'll be forced to tell Colin about your extracurricular evening activities."

And that was the last straw. He touched a nerve, and he knew it. "We're done."

"Have it your way. But I won't be here for you to crawl back to when you decide you have an itch. I'm done with the games."

And so was I. That we could agree on.

Liam spun around. With forceful strides, he walked back toward the compound, but not before he brushed shoulders with Zavier. "She's your problem now," Liam spat, casting a glare in my direction before disappearing inside.

Fan-freaking-tastic.

At least the dirty deed was done. Hopefully with some space and time, we might be able to salvage our friendship. I didn't want to lose someone else I cared about. And maybe I should have thought about that before I let things cross the line, but Liam had been there when I needed someone.

Zavier's brows rose. "You want to tell me what that was all about?"

I sighed. "Not really."

"Why do I get the feeling this job is about to get dangerous?"

"Because you're starting to understand me. I'm a magnet for death and heartache." I wasn't looking for sympathy or a shoulder to cry on. I wanted the misery that curled inside me. Unless Zavier was bringing the dark cloud as company, he better keep his opinion to himself.

CHAPTER 7

I n the dark green shadows of the deep woods, an hour before midnight, the coven met in secret. The dilemma was how I was going to get there tonight. Just shy of two hours before I was supposed to be sneaking out the small opening in the fence, I was in my room, wearing the floor down with my pacing.

"Why couldn't he be human like the other wardens?" I grumbled.

I took a sip from the glass of wine to calm my nerves, and set it back down on the little table near my bed. *Why the hell am I so frazzled? Because you're afraid he will catch you, and everything you've been working for will be for naught.*

Damn right I was.

And I couldn't let that happen.

So what was I going to do to ensure Zavier didn't know I had slipped out in the middle of the night?

It helped to have a focus, a goal. One task at a time.

As I paced back and forth, I racked my brain, searching for a rune or incantation I hadn't thought of before. The was good chance the only way I was getting out of this room was climbing over the terrace and scaling the walls of the compound.

I'd rather not go splat on the ground, but it was getting to the point where I didn't see I had any other options.

Colin would kill me if he found out.

A risk I might have to take.

Since magic seemed out of the question, I was going to rely on a simple tactic. Female distraction. Tulip.

She had a way with men, and I was betting Zavier would be no different. If she could keep him occupied, it would give me enough time to slip down the hall with a cloaking spell, praying he couldn't see through all my charms.

I conjured the summoning spell, something Tulip and I had done since childhood. Hopefully, she wasn't otherwise engaged. It had never been a problem when we were younger, but now, out of respect for her privacy, I only did it when necessary.

Like now.

In less than a minute, Tulip's pretty face materialized in my bedroom. I was glad to see she was fully dressed. She had her hands on her hips as she waited for the spell to complete, entirely transferring her physical form from one place to another.

Tulip lips thinned into a straight line. "Are you dying? You better be dying."

"Not yet, but I need your help." I gave her the quick rundown of what I needed. She might not have been pleased, but she was someone I could always count on to come through when it mattered most.

"You owe me," Tulip mumbled.

I rolled my eyes. "Please, you've been dying to flirt with him. I'm doing you a favor."

"Maybe, but I've seen the look in your eyes, and you're worried, which makes me worried. And I know you. Zavier has your interest, whether you want to admit it, so why would I stand in your way?"

"I don't have time to get tangled into another mess."

"Uh-huh. If you say so." Her fingers combed through her curls. "I didn't even have time to do my hair."

"Thank you." I engulfed her in a quick hug.

I waited until I heard her giggling voice before flipping the hood of the dark cloak over my head, covering the gleam of my auburn hair, and setting forth. The rune at my wrist cloaked me invisible as I snuck out of the compound and through the little opening in the fence.

Soon, the longest day would become the shortest night of the solstice. And unlike my ancestors, there would be no celebration, no festival of growth, or circle of thanks to the goddess Litha.

As I walked through the dense woods, a sensation trickled up my spine. The only sounds were my soft footsteps and the whistling of the wind, but still, awareness that someone was watching me remained. I pushed forward, almost to the little cottage.

I'd been following impulse and instinct since I turned fifteen, just after I learned the truth of what had happened to my mother. I waited for the anger and the need for justice to gradually subside. The thing was, it never did. If anything, as the years went by, the seed for revenge only festered.

Certain I was being paranoid, I hurried my strides. Within minutes, the little vine-covered cottage came into view. I sighed, bounding up the creaky and warped wooden steps. At one time, it had probably been a cute little yellow getaway nestled in the woods. Now, it was forgotten and neglected, making it the perfect little hideaway.

I gave three knocks on the door, and glanced over my shoulder one last time while I waited for someone to answer. The feeling of being followed returned, but as I scoured the woods, I saw nothing.

"Oh hey, it's the crazy witch."

I couldn't contain the smirk. Jenna Athens stood on the other side of the door, glaring at me. "Wow. How unoriginal, but then again, Jenna, I'd expect nothing less from you."

Jenna had legs that went on for miles, and beautiful whitish-gold hair that framed an angelic face, but there was nothing innocent about her. "Bitch."

"Skank," I replied.

Bright baby-blue eyes danced as they met mine. Jenna folded her arms, leaned a shoulder against the doorframe, and crossed her killer legs at the ankles. "Remind me again why we allowed you into our coven?"

Jenna and I had a bit of a history. We had a truce for the sake of the coven, but it was a shaky truce that dangled by a thread. "Because I have more power in my pinkie than you have in your entire body." I stepped to the side and swept into the small room.

"Right. There's that," she said, swinging the door shut.

The walls were made of wood, painted white to cut down on some of the rawness. In the center was a circular rug with numerous decorative pillows to sit on. Tall pillared candles lined against the walls, casting a soft, flickering glow over the room. The air was scented with vanilla and pine.

Let the magic begin.

The coven was made up of five witches, myself included.

Abbey, Bailey, and Raine were sitting on the rug in a semi-circle. Only two spots left to complete the circle. Each one of us were bound to magic, and much like those who had met so many years in an attempt to cure vampirism, we now met to stop the very things our ancestors had tried to help.

Irony.

"Who brought the wine?" I asked, dropping the cloak off my head.

Bailey held up not one, but two bottles, clinging them together at the base. The wine was another ritual, one used to take the edge off the kind of magic we performed deep in the woods.

Raine smiled, her legs curled cozily underneath her. An oversized knit sweater in raspberry dwarfed her petite frame. "We weren't sure you were coming."

The spell needed all five elements to balance and protect. Without one, the risk of something going wrong increased tenfold. Magic had a price. It wasn't to be taken lightly. There was an order in which things needed to be done.

"Colin decided it was time for a guard change, and my new warden isn't as susceptible to my charms as Liam was," I informed.

"Oooh. Do tell," Abbey purred like a cat, which was fitting. She had amber eyes that often took on a feline ambiance. "Is he single? Does he dig witches?"

"How would I know?" I shrugged, taking a seat on the woven rug. "We haven't talked about his sexual preferences."

"You know what that means, girls. She's got it bad. What is with you and your wardens?" Jenna asked. "Do you have a dominance fetish?"

I rolled my eyes. "Can we just get this started? I don't have all night like the rest of you."

Jenna smirked. She lived to razz me. "Right. We have to get Cinderella back to the castle before midnight strikes."

Our hands joined, one by one, awaking the elements. Fire ringed around earth, and the wind lifted the flames high as the mist of smoke rose, our spirits united.

"This is our place, a place conjured from knowledge and hope. Power born and passed down to us." My voice rang out clear and rich as we bound the circle, linking our souls, our powers with the elements. The air began to tingle. "Together, we twine our gifts, combine our souls, vanquish our doubts, and conquer our fears. Hearts and minds, open and free. This I do willingly."

"As do I," Abbey responded.

And one after the other, the others recited, until the circle was completed.

Then the fun began.

The vision sucked us all under at once, but as long as none of us broke the circle, we'd be safe. It was when the link was severed that mind and spirit got jumbled, making the trip back to the body a difficult and unpleasant experience.

I trusted the four other girls with my life, even if we didn't always get along or see eye to eye, but when it came to coven creed, we supported one another. We were sisters.

The process was sort of like traveling, but only in spirit, which also made detection of the invasion nearly impossible, unless there was another witch about.

Shadows, grey as smoke, ringed the edges of my vision. I could sense each of the others, their presence a comfort, familiar. When the fog cleared, I was staring at three figures, ringed inside a circle of blood. A brunette with short, choppy hair stood over a man, who cowered at her feet. Her lips curved into a seductive sneer, blood smeared on her mouth like it was bold crimson lipstick.

A dark violence shimmered in the air around her that had alarm squeezing in my chest.

Lilith—the self-proclaimed queen of vampires.

She was the oldest Bitten in Frisco Bay, and what I considered the most dangerous. It had been her fangs that had ripped the life from my mother, and it would be by my hand that would end the she-devil vampire.

But what concerned me was the plot she has conspiring to track down the witches in the Bay to use them for various purposes. Although, there were many benefits from the Rift, like daywalking and sustaining on human food, their desire for blood and power was a commanding hunger that wasn't satisfied with the measly offerings from humans or animals. For a vampire, there wasn't a more potent blood than that of a witch, and those vampires who were old enough to remember the immense pleasure longed for a taste. It was like a forbidden fruit, sweet and succulent.

"Did you find me a witch, one with the blood of a descendant?" Lilith asked the vampire to her right.

His hair was as dark as a moonless night, pulled back into a low ponytail at the nape of his neck. There was a shifty nervousness to his light sapphire eyes. "We haven't been able to locate one yet, but we will."

It was Lilith's son Aeron. He was a real heartless asshole, much like his wicked mother. The pair frightened me and my circle, and the rising of unease trickled through our bond.

The sneer on her lips dropped, and her hand shot out, faster than my eyes could follow, securing around the human's neck. She pulled him to his feet, never easing up on her grip. The man gasped, struggling for air, his face draining of blood.

Her gaze shifted sideways toward her son. "My patience is running thin, Aeron. For each day it takes, I will kill one of your little pets." To prove her point, Lilith extended one dagger-like nail and sliced it across the human's throat. His eyes went wide, a gurgle bubbling from his mouth a moment before he was tossed to the floor like trash.

Everything inside me strained to do something. Anything.

Aeron hissed, his fangs extending in rage, the lean muscles in his arms tightening. "Was that necessary? We were just getting to know each other."

"The courtship is over, and dinner is served."

I could smell death. It lingered in the air.

"I find my appetite is not what it was," he replied drolly, regardless that the veins surrounding his eyes darkened with hunger.

"If you spent half as much time knocking up witches as you do with your male consorts, we might have already found what we've been searching for," she spat before spinning around, her dark purple robes swishing as she dismissed her son.

Blood rushed and roared in my head, pulsing in time with my thumping heart. The spell was coming to an end, our power wavering. The five of us were back inside the little cottage, staring into one another's pale faces. Each time the spell was performed, we learned a little bit more about what that bitch was planning. If we could stay a step ahead, we would have the advantage. The problem was this kind of magic was draining, and we could never hold onto it for prolonged periods, not without risking each other.

"We must do something. We can't sit here as more and more humans are sacrificed." Outrage was ever present in my voice.

"Is there no other way?" Abbey, the peacemaker, asked.

"If there is another, I can't see it, but what I do see is they will hunt us down like cattle, slaughter us for the power they crave. It will not end with one or two deaths. Skylar is right. I have seen it." Jenna was a seer as well as a pain in the ass. Her visions weren't to be taken lightly.

There was sorrow in my voice, but behind it was a firm purpose. "She is searching for all of us, and the golden prize, a witch with the blood of one of the originals. We need to be more cautious. She can't get her hands on any of us. The outcome would be catastrophic."

"Lilith can go to the devil before I let her find any of us," Jenna swore, fire burning in her eyes. "I won't be a breeding machine for her clan of bloodsuckers."

"God, I need a drink," Bailey said, pushing to her feet. Her round cheeks were flushed.

I couldn't agree more. It was time to break out another bottle of wine. We all felt it—we were running out of time. The vampires were gathering their ranks, and it could be any day that Lilith decided to strike. It was more than a war or prepopulating their numbers. She wanted to reverse what the Rift witches had done, but that hadn't gone so well the first time. I shuddered to think what would happen to Frisco Bay if another spell of that magnitude was cast.

Later, feeling a little buzzed from the wine, I threw the cloak over my head, hiding my face, and slipped back out into the night. After what I'd seen, my body was on edge. For the first time, I understood why my overprotective brother never relented on his demand I be protected. The other girls didn't have a warden to look out for them. Then again, neither of them was a direct descendant of a Rift witch.

She was after me, and I wanted Lilith dead.

I made it a couple of feet when something—correction—someone stepped out from behind a tree. The person grabbed a hold of me.

An arm curled around my stomach, just below my breasts and tugged me back against them. Before I could catch my breath or curse the perpetrator, I was off my feet, being taken behind a rundown shack. A hand clamped over my mouth, and all the hours of self-defense my brother taught kicked in.

I brought my elbow forward, planning to use my weight and throw us to the ground.

"I wouldn't do that if I were you," whispered a voice directly in my ear. "Be a good girl and don't scream. I'm going to release my hand, but I also don't want to alert every vampire within a mile. Do you understand?"

There was something familiar about the voice, but I didn't dwell on it. My mind was already conjuring how much pain I was going to cause him the moment he set me free. I nodded, letting him know I wouldn't scream, but he hadn't said anything about kicking his ass.

He released his arm from around my upper stomach. Without hesitation, I spun around. My gaze locked onto a pair of starlight eyes.

CHAPTER 8

"**W**hat the hell, Zavier?" I whispered. Every muscle in my body tensed when I realized who my kidnapper was.

A lopsided grin curled on his lips as he caught my wrists in the air. I had been aiming for his face. "You forgot to tell me we were going out tonight."

I yanked on my hands, setting them free from his grip. "Are you sure? I swear I told you. Maybe you need to listen more, or maybe you were preoccupied."

"Yes, thank you for the gift, but Tulip isn't my type. And as much as I would love to argue with you, we have company."

I blew out a breath that was part relieved and part irritated before leaning against the tattered side of the building. "Was it necessary to scare the shit out of me?"

He shot me a grin complete with dimples. "I'd apologize, but I'm not sorry. Besides, you were about to make a huge mistake."

"You mean by not kicking your ass? I still might, you know. The night's not over."

He shook his head. "I can think of better use of your energy."

I scrunched my nose. "Does everything you say end in a phrase about sex?"

Dark brows lifted. "Now who's the one with the dirty mind?"

"Only because you put it there," I spat.

"Did I?"

I whacked him on the shoulder. The truth was I'd never been so glad to see him. By no means would I'd admit that to anyone but myself. The odds of me being abducted by the vampire queen got cut in half, or less if Zavier was as good as he claimed. I had yet to see him in action, and I was too damn tired to pay attention to his skills tonight.

"How did you know where to find me?" I asked, glancing sideways at him.

"I followed you."

My mouth dropped. "You followed an invisible person. Wow. I thought I was crazy."

He smirked. "Crazy loves company."

Damn those dimples. Why couldn't he have the face of an ogre? "And you didn't try to stop me?"

He shrugged. "I figured if you were going to such lengths to sneak out, then it must be important."

"And you wanted to spy on me?" I added. It was hard to believe I was huddled behind a shed having this discussion with Zavier. I was curious to see what the outcome was going to be. If he threatened to tell my brother…I couldn't be held responsible for my actions.

He crossed his arms, twinkling eyes looking down at me. "You're seriously hung up on the stalker theory."

"If the shoe fits."

He shook his head. "It took guts coming out here alone, but you don't lack bravado. What you lack is common sense."

"What makes you so sure?"

"The moment you stepped into these woods, you made a mistake. And I'm guessing this isn't the first time you've met with those other four witches, is it?"

Floored, all I could do was stare at him for a minute, and then my tongue returned with a vengeance. "*That* is none of your business. By the way, I don't make mistakes, asshole. And I don't need you."

"I'm a lot of things, including an asshole probably, but tonight, I'm your fucking knight in shining armor." His voice had risen to match mine, no longer doing the forced whisper.

I shoved at a piece of hair that had fallen into my face. "Wow. You want a freaking cookie? How about I bake you a cake?"

He blinked. "I didn't know you could bake."

"Go jump off a cliff."

He dipped his chin and stretched his head to the side as if he heard something. "Stay behind me," he ordered.

I opened my mouth, but the glare in his eyes struck me silent. There was something in the way he went from teasing to dangerous warden that sent off a warning signal inside me. Now was not the time to test him.

"We need to go," he told me curtly.

Cold shivers navigated down my spinal cord, and every nerve ending in my body fired a rush of cautionary sensations. Zavier's hand slipped into mine as he moved soundlessly with me at his back. He'd only taken a few steps before he halted.

I caught a glimpse of disheveled mocha hair and a

hunched-over figure. A vampire was having a late-night snack on a human, slurping the woman's blood and slowly stripping away her life, until there was nothing but an empty shell left.

Fury rose within me as swiftly as the dense fog off the sea. My fingers curled into fists, red hot anger filling my veins. I was focused entirely on the vampire as I put one foot in front of the other and stalked forward.

"Hey bloodsucker, the feast is over. She isn't an all-you-can-eat buffet." Magic radiated from my fingertips. I wasn't sure what came over me, but after what I'd witnessed tonight and years of pent-up rage, I lost it.

"Christ," Zavier swore.

The vampire's head snapped up, blood dripping from his fangs. A deep line of crimson trickled from the woman's neck onto the ground. He gave a seething hiss at having his dinner interrupted. No one liked to be disturbed during a meal.

Heart pounding, I launched myself forward. Zavier did as well, once again putting himself in front of me.

"What are you doing?" he hissed between his teeth.

"Getting some justice," I growled, my eyes focused on the leech. Never lose track of them, the number-one rule.

"Is that what you call this?" Zavier cracked his neck. "Well then, I guess we better get on with it."

I couldn't believe he was going to help me kick this vampire's ass. He was such a quandary. From the corner of my eyes, I looked at the warden. He was serious. This was a different approach, and I liked it. After I engaged the rune on my shoulder, the mark lit up, glowing white in the dark.

"Witch," the vampire hissed.

"Wow, he speaks."

Zavier chuckled.

Releasing the woman, the vampire flashed to his feet. "Oh honey, I can do a whole lot more than talk. Let me take care of him and I'll show you."

"Can't wait," I said with genuine anticipation. I wanted to hit something. This vampire's face would do just fine.

"Do you bait everyone you cross paths with?" Zavier grumbled.

"Don't tell me you're afraid of a little vampire. I thought you were supposed to be a big, bad warden."

"One is no sweat, but where there is one, there are more. Trust me, this guy is not alone."

"That's right." The vampire lurched forward, suddenly in my face. I blinked, and two other vampires dropped down on either side of Zavier, another man with blond hair and a female who could have been his twin. Freaky. I was getting some incestual vibes from them.

The scowl on Zavier's face was fierce and displeased. He wanted to tell me he told me so. I had a feeling I was going to be paying for this later...once we made it out alive. "You don't want to do this. Trust me. This woman is under my protection," Zavier barked.

"She's a witch. And we have our own orders," the vampire said, disregarding Zavier's warning.

"Your orders mean very little to me. I'm going to give you one more chance to walk away before I make sure you never see the light of another day."

"What you don't understand, warden, is if I don't bring her back with me, I'm dead. So I've got nothing to lose."

And that made the vampire dangerous.

"She isn't going anywhere, but you three are going to hell," Zavier thundered.

I backed away as the vampire's hand shot at me. From the corner of my eye, I saw Zavier upper cut the female vampire, snapping her head back. She went down like a bag of rocks.

I threw out my hand, an orb of green magic zooming through the air, zeroing on the vampire. The electric ball of light smacked him in the gut, a inch above making it nearly impossible for him to have kids, not that I was going to let the bastard live. He threatened me, and for that, I'd have his life.

The magic would only stun him, but the stake I'd hidden in my boot would do so much more. I bent down, grabbing the wooden hilt and throwing it. The small weapon spun in the air, hitting the vampire in the heart, sinking deep. A startled look crossed his face, and as the composite of the stake worked its wonder, he disappeared in a flash of blinding light.

A hand latched onto my ankle and yanked. There was a third burst of light as I tumbled to the ground, but someone cushioned my fall. Zavier. He stared at me. "I'm not sure if I should be horrified or impressed."

I heaved a breath I didn't know I'd been holding. "Ditto."

Shoulders still tense, Zavier lowered his chin and met my gaze. There was an illuminating glow to his eyes. "Both. I'm not someone to be tampered with. It would do for you to remember that the next time you go sneaking off alone. I told you it wasn't safe."

"And I told you I can take care of myself," I huffed.

"So you did. Not bad, minx, but how about we make a deal? Next time you want to go sneaking off into the woods, you tell me first, that way I can make sure I bring more than one stake."

I simmered down. "You're not going to go squealing to Colin?"

"I'm to keep you safe, not gossip or tattle. What you do is your own business. You're a big girl, but it would make my job easier if I knew ahead of time what we were getting into."

"Whatever. Let me go."

"Newsflash, sweetheart, you're sitting on me, and if you slip about an inch or so down, things are either going to be awkward...or interesting," he added. His lips slowly curled as he lifted a brow. "Could be fun."

I rolled my eyes. "Shut up. I'm not a plaything."

He lifted both hands in the air on either side of him, his gaze traveling over my body before flicking up. "Who said I'm playing?"

I put a palm to his chest, intending to push myself to my feet, but I gasped as his hand wrapped around my wrist, hauling me against his chest. I turned my bewildered stare back on Zavier, the air catching in my lungs. He took a deep breath, and I realized my chest was pressed to his so close I could feel his heart beating.

His hand fell loosely around my waist, and a heady rush trilled through my body. My fingers bunched on his shirt. To my surprise, they wanted to tug him closer, as if they had a mind of their own. The knowledge had my stomach muscles tightening. Maybe it was the adrenaline rush from the fight with the vampires, but holy crap. I was feeling a mad case of insta-lust.

What was wrong with me? Better question—what the hell was going on with my body?

I had just ended things with Liam, and here I was, having not-so-innocent thoughts about another guy. Never had I felt this kind of intense level of attraction, and I wasn't sure I was ready for it, no matter what my body was saying.

Flattening my hands, I shoved at the center of his chest and pushed to my feet. "Fun's over."

Zavier was bad news all right.

CHAPTER 9

I went to bed all churned up inside, thanks to Zavier and Lilith. The type of spell my coven performed tonight usually left my body in a state of exhaustion that put me in a dreamless coma-like slumber, but as my head hit the pillow and I drifted off, the dreams of the past came.

Bats swarmed over the mouth of the cave, the swirling and wrestling of their wings stirred in the otherwise eerily calm night. Seeing the Bay as it had been over fifty years ago was always a shock. It was almost unrecognizable, the city lights in the distance so vibrant and bright, but here at the edge of the world, the vast ocean slapped against the cliffs, and it was nestled into the side of the rock that the Rift witches gathered.

Their voices carried in the wind, candles flickering from the opening, casting shadows that appeared as giants. "In blood taken. In magic given. So we may live. So the undead may rise. No longer bound by thirst. No longer feared by death." The Rift witches chanted, the words trailing off by the hiss and roll of the surf.

I moved closer, straining to hear the words that had

destroyed the world, but from the darkness, a woman formed, her hair as black as night. Robes the same color of her hair swirled around her. She put a finger to her lips, a smile of terrible beauty.

Lilith.

"I have waited for you." Bats swooped and squawked as she lifted her hand toward my face, but her voice rang over the chaos, clear and strong.

I jerked my head out of her reach, and a bat dived at me.

In a movement of liquid blur, Lilith grasped my chin, holding my face steady in her clutch. Our eyes met, and I refused to blink or look away. I wouldn't show her the fear she sought. "Ah yes, my dear, you have the strength I seek, but do you also have the power?"

"You will get nothing from me but your death," I spat, letting the words fly from my mouth with malice.

She laughed, a chilling sound that sent shivers down my arms. "Until then, I'll have a taste and see."

I didn't have a chance to react. Her fangs extended as she grabbed my wrist, sinking them into my flesh. The sting was quick, and it swiftly gave way to a feeling equivalent to euphoria as the venom on her fangs mixed with my blood.

"It's warm," she said, licking a drop of crimson delicately from the side of her lips as if it was a dab of ice cream. "Your power is ancient…and very tasty. Through your power is the path to redemption. I've been searching for you far too long. What is your name?"

She was a whack-job if she thought I would voluntarily give her my name. "Death."

The curve of her lips never wavered, regardless of the darkness that jumped into her glowing eyes. "Your wit is only amusing for so long."

"It isn't meant to amuse, but to warn."

She shook her head. "Come to me, and I will reward you. All I ask is for a little of your blood and a pinch of magic. I can give you more power than you've ever felt. I can show you how."

I snorted. "I'd rather jump off a cliff."

A bloodcurdling scream tore through the night. It was drowned out by the rapid beating of wings. My hands flew to cover my face as I ducked, shielding myself. I gasped at the quick pain as something sliced my arm. Cradling it, I felt the warm, wet flow of my own blood drip to the ground, splattering over the gritty sand.

The earth under my feet shook.

I must have pissed her off. Good.

As satisfying as the knowledge was, it didn't help me in my current predicament. There was something very real about this dream, and although it was of the past, Lilith was very much the present.

A storm rolled in over the cliffs, gushing winds of frost that struck my face in sharp slaps. Lightning spat from the sky, an angry fire that slammed against the crack of thunder. The candles from the cave extinguished, leaving the bluffs in utter darkness.

There was a gleeful kind of mean in the air, a sizzle of temper and spite that rippled with power—a power Lilith shouldn't have—magic.

What the hell?

But that wasn't my immediate concern. In the pitch black of night, I could no longer find my way. I didn't know which direction was home. There was nothing to guide me back, and I begin to panic. Blind, desperate, and utterly alone, everything the vampire queen wanted—to isolate me until I gave in.

I refused.

Through the darkness came a light, and a feeling like a pair of strong arms wrapping around me. I was enclosed in a blanket of warmth and security, the white glow slowly gaining ground, drowning out the fear, the violent storm, and the vampire who was darkness incarnate. Lilith screamed, lunging at me in one last attempt to keep me within her nightmare, but the light of hope was too strong. The dream and the fear faded like smoke in the fog, yet the wariness of what had happened lingered as I slept.

❧

THERE WAS one thing I didn't expect when I woke up in the morning. Zavier Cross in my bed. Part of my brain couldn't fathom what he was doing lying beside me with a twinkle in his silver eyes.

Am I dreaming? Did I drink last night?

His lips curved into a rather devastating smile that showed off his dimples.

Definitely not dreaming. I couldn't dream up that smirk, but through the haze of being still groggy, memories of the dream filtered through. Lilith. The Rift witches. Bats. Zavier had not been in the dream, and I was positive he hadn't been in my bed as I had drifted off last night, so why he was here now?

Several dark locks fell across his forehead that made my fingers itch to brush them aside. What was going on inside me? My eyes got hung up on his lips, and I couldn't seem to look away.

A flush trickled between my breasts, spreading to my belly,

and then lower. Wickedness. It was the first word that came to mind.

Holy crap. I wanted Zavier to touch me. However, it was completely wrong, and I didn't need another entanglement with a warden. The first one hadn't ended so well, but the mere thought of his touch on my skin caused my body to arch into him.

Zavier's hand was at my hip. It slowly began to inch down my thigh. I did nothing to stop him, my uneven breaths only encouraging him. There was no mistaking the desire that clouded his eyes. I shuddered as the tips of his fingers caressed along the edge of my inner thigh, and my head fell back against the pillow.

What was happening to me? It was as if someone else had taken over my body, a sex-crazed harlot who was screaming at me to lean up and kiss those full lips, to wipe off that cocky smirk.

It was becoming an annoying habit—Zavier knowing what I wanted without my having to utter a word. He pressed a light kiss to the corner of my mouth, testing the waters. His chest rose heavily in time with mine.

Was I letting this happen?

My tongued ran over my lips, eager to taste him again. It would be a good time to try to get a read on his essence, my mind rationalized. I was willing to grasp at any excuse to kiss him. It was pathetic, but I hated there was an attraction. No matter how much I ignored it, it only grew stronger.

Zavier's eyes stayed on mine as all this went through my head, and the degree of desire that flourished sent a tingling thrill within me. I lost myself in those damn eyes. He pulled me in and took my lips, sweeping me under. And this time, the storm broke over me in wild lightning.

I embraced it.

My body naturally leaned toward him, seeking his warmth. His body was like a summer night, the winds breathing the air of the coast over the darkness.

Desire fluttered in my belly like a dozen velvet butterfly wings. This was insane. Everywhere he touched sparked. His hand trailed from my thigh back to my hip and up my side, lingering just under my breast. The rush of my pulse sent a warning to my brain. Things were spinning out of control too fast. I'd always been a master over my own body and feelings, but what was happening now was foreign—just like Zavier.

As before, I got sense of who he was, but it could be that my own desire was keeping me from being able to get any real information about the man. I was in so much trouble.

I wanted my hands on him, on flesh, on muscle. My fingers edged to the hem of his pants, surprised he was wearing any, but he had forgone a shirt. His teeth grazed lightly down my throat as my fingers explored the hard planes of his stomach. Muscles bunched under my touch. There was a sweetness to the way he kissed as Zavier reclaimed my lips, slow and deep, until I could do nothing but melt into him. It was a dangerous concoction he brewed, seducing us both.

He smelled of the sea and tasted like a honey elixir. Under his hands, he made my skin feel as soft as a rose petal.

I wanted to leap in, ride the storm he created until the end, no matter where it took me. But the risk, and the pain…I was no stranger to pain of the heart, and based on what he could make me feel with a few swoon-worthy kisses, Zavier had the power to shatter my heart beyond repair. It was already damaged—I was damaged. The last thing I needed was a complication. There were plenty of those already.

Pressing a hand to his chest, I pulled back, giving us both

air. His eyes locked on mine, and I swore I saw something—the swirling of magic—wild and untamed.

"Good morning," he murmured, his husky voice dancing over my cheek as a hot, dangerous glint shifted into humor.

I struggled to find my balance, the reality of what had transpired between us coming into focus. "What are you doing in my bed?"

He lifted on an elbow and looked down at me. "Don't you remember? You were calling out my name in the middle of the night."

I hadn't been able to pry anything from the kiss. Zavier was still as much a mystery to me as ever. "I was not."

A single brow arched. "Are you sure about that?"

I bit my lip, tasting him there. The thing was where Zavier was concerned, I wasn't certain of anything. "That makes no sense. I had a dream, but why would I call for you? I don't even like you."

The pad of his thumb swept over my bottom lip as he captured my gaze. "Do you need me to show you again how much you *don't* like me?"

I swatted his hand away from my face, going into bitch mode. The last thing I needed was a reminder of being in his arms, when I was doing my damnedest to forget it ever happened. "You're a dick."

His lips curled. "You know, you're not the first girl to tell me so."

I shot my nose into the air. "Shocker. This never happened." I slipped out of the bed, leaving him stretched out across the sheets. "Next time you think you hear me cry in the middle of the night, try the chair in the corner." Without saying goodbye, I slipped into the bathroom.

✥

THOUGH IT WAS BARELY DAWN, I made my way down to the kitchen. I was Cranky McCranky-Pants, only running on a few hours of sleep and suppressing my need to play hockey tonsil with Zavier. Mornings weren't my thing. I didn't understand anyone who got up at the butt crack of dawn on purpose.

The kitchen wasn't empty when I walked through. Colin was leaning against the industrial counter with an apple in his hand, dressed in the dark warden uniform. "You look like crap today," he said, watching me as I went to the pantry.

"Thanks, bro. I feel even better now."

He chuckled. "Late night?"

My eyes snapped over to him. "No. Why? What did you hear?"

Might not have been the smartest reaction. Now Colin was suspicious, his gaze narrowing at me, and then to Zavier, who had come in and was quietly helping himself to breakfast. "Nothing. Should I have? What shenanigans did you get yourself into?" Colin shifted so his body faced me.

I exhaled. So Zavier hadn't ratted me out. He kept his word. Wow. Color me shocked. "I've not gotten myself into anything. I've spent some time getting to know the warden you assigned me."

He took a bite out of his apple. "What do you mean by *getting to know*?"

"I'm not a slut, Colin. Give me some credit. Just because I had a fling with Liam doesn't mean I sleep around."

"Geez, Sky. What crawled up your ass? I wasn't implying you were anything, but since you brought it up… You do tend to bewitch my friends."

"Zavier is a friend?" I asked. I thought I knew all my brother's friends. I was positive Zavier hadn't been part of the guards. If he'd gone through training here, I would have remembered him. He had a face that was unforgettable, and yet, Colin made it sound as if they had history.

Colin leaned back and folded his arms. "You know I wouldn't assign someone I didn't personally trust with my life. Zavier and I trained together. He is one of the best, if not the best warden I've ever seen."

He was laying it on thick. I dropped into a chair, munching on the granola I grabbed from the cupboard. "Sounds like someone has a man crush."

"What is with you and Liam? Did you guys have a fight or something? The two of you are pricklier than a desert cactus."

"You could say that." My brother had the ability to make me feel normal…a rare feeling. Colin and I used to be close, but lately, we'd grown distant, each caught up in our own lives and problems.

And that sucked. I missed him.

He leaned on the counter. "Skylar, what did you do?"

I frowned. "Why does it have to be my fault?"

He gave me that brotherly stern glare.

"Fine. You got me." I leaned back in the chair, picking at the granola I'd chosen for breakfast. "I told him I didn't think we should see each other anymore."

"Wow. But that's probably for the best."

"Has there been a second Rift I'm unaware of? What did you do with my brother?"

He waved his apple in the air. "Hardy-har-har. It was no secret I didn't approve, and it explains his piss-poor mood."

"How is he?" Liam and I hadn't spoken since the other night. He was avoiding me, and I couldn't blame him. I was doing a bit of avoiding myself.

Thoughtful lines crinkled at the corners of his eyes. "Putting on a brave face, but I knew something was eating at him, and now I know what. Makes sense why he has been spending extra time in the combat room."

I groaned. "Colin, I've made a mess of this. I never wanted to hurt Liam."

"I know. It hasn't been easy for you." Colin tossed an apple from the basket to me. "Don't worry about Liam. You know how he gets. Give him a few days to lick his wounded pride, but things will get back to the way they were. Besides, he'll be busy over the next few days."

I wished I had Colin's confidence. "What happened?" There was a spark of sadness in Colin's eyes that he quickly tried to hide from me, but he hadn't been quick enough.

"There was another attack in town yesterday."

Zavier stiffened from his lounging place in the corner. This was news to him as well.

The apple was halfway to my mouth when my hand paused. "How many?"

Colin heaved a heavy sigh before running a hand through his shaggy hair. Someone was in dire need of a trim. "At least three that we know of. Maybe more."

"Things are escalating, Colin. We need to do something about it. We can't let them take innocent people. No one feels safe anymore, especially now that the sunlight has very little effect on them since the Rift."

"Sky, you're telling me facts I already know. I'm working on it. That's all you need to worry about."

Of course. Colin would take care of it alone. Without his little sister's help, because sheltering me always came first. Sometimes I wanted to scream. When was he going to wake up and see I wasn't a fragile little girl he had to constantly protect? I'd seen what evil looked like. Keeping me guarded wasn't going to change the past.

I understood the responsibility of safeguarding the people of Frisco Bay was a heavy burden, and it was in Colin's nature to defend. He respected laws and order, unlike someone else I knew.

CHAPTER 10

The furnishings were sparse within the compound, as was common in the Bay. The Rift left District Fourteen in shambles. A simple sofa that desperately needed recovering sat in the corner of the main room, along with a cushioned chair and a scatter of tables.

I needed a moment alone to gather myself, but it was impossible with Zavier's stormy eyes watching my every move. He made me feel quivery and no longer empty.

I had to keep my mind focused on other things like work, inventory for the shop, what I was going to eat for lunch. If I didn't, my mind wandered to Zavier and what happened this morning.

Had I really called out to him? He had come into my room and comforted me? It was what I assumed he had done. I thought about the dream and the bright light at the end that had saved me. Could that have been Zavier?

What a crazy notion.

I found myself staring off, my thoughts getting away from me.

Time to be practical. There was evil in the works, and Lilith was fighting dirty in her search for a witch. We needed to take precautions. I thought about telling Colin what I'd seen, but knowing my brother, I crossed it off my list. I would end up with twice as many details tailing me. No thank you. Zavier was like ten egotistical wardens wrapped in one glorious body.

My brother was a witch, but he didn't practice magic. He preferred using his fists and wits to fight his battles. I understood that. Respected it even. What I didn't understand was Zavier. Or what he made me feel.

"What put the worry in your eyes?"

Zavier's voice behind me pulled me out of my head, and I turned around. I couldn't very well tell him it was him I'd been thinking about, so I went with the obvious answer. "The dream I had last night."

Zavier straightened as his eyes met mine. "Tell me what you saw."

I tilted my head to the side. "For a second, you had me convinced you believed in dream weaving."

His expression never wavered. "There are things in this world I'll never understand, like how you were ever into Liam."

I frowned.

"But only a fool ignores what he doesn't understand. I'm no fool, minx. Magic is more than tricks and glamour. And you're more than a pretty face. You're smart and clever."

Wow. Two compliments at once. I might fall dead from shock. It was strange opening up to him. For so long, I'd kept this part of my life a secret, but somehow, in a brief time, Zavier had managed to weasel his way into the hidden layers I kept locked away. I bit my lip, contemplating how much further I wanted to pull Zavier in. I still had trust issues, yet I found that I wanted someone to talk with.

Running a hand through my hair, I made the decision, my shoulders relaxing. "I'm not entirely sure what happened. The dream started out as many of them have since my mother died. Visions of the past, her memories."

His features softened. "You get glimpses of before the Rift?"

I nodded. "I believe that's what they are. I could hear chanting from a cave on the bluffs, the Rift witches. The sea was rolling in and out on the coast, and a swarm of bats dived from the mouth of the cave. It all felt so real, as if I were there. I drew closer to the flickering of candles in the cave, and Lilith showed up."

"Lilith?" Zavier echoed. "The vampire queen?"

"Is there another one?"

"Let's hope not," he mumbled.

He echoed my sentiment exactly. "Things took a turn for the dark side once she appeared."

"Did she try to hurt you?" He jumped to the right conclusion, his eyes narrowing with worry.

I lifted my hand and turned my wrist, glancing at the inside where she had helped herself to a sampling of my blood. I hadn't noticed it before, but there were two fresh fang marks. "That can't be," I muttered, feeling the room spin.

Zavier suddenly closed the space between us. I wasn't sure how he moved so fast, but his hand flashed out, grasping my wrist and causing tingles to radiate over my skin. "She did this? She bit you?" The pad of his thumb glided over the twin marks that ran along the vein.

"I-I don't know. It was a dream." My eyes flicked to his, relieved to see not a single look of judgment. "How could this be real? She took a little of my blood. If this had been magic—a spell—it was of the dark arts."

"That we can agree on. You're going to need wards to protect your dreams." His fingers still held my wrist, and he lifted my arm. "These runes aren't going to be enough to keep Lilith out."

I arched a brow. "You know a lot about magic for a human. Not to mention, you shouldn't be able to see my runes."

"I told you I was full of surprises. Believe it or not, I grew up with a witch."

A wisp of hair fell over my face. "Colin said you trained together. I don't remember ever seeing you."

"I remember you."

"Every part of that sentence horrifies me."

He twirled the stray curl around his finger. "Your hair was more red than brown then. Always following Colin and Liam around, getting into more trouble than they could get you out of. They were very protective of you, even then."

I swallowed. "You have no magic in your blood. I would know."

He was no longer touching me, and I couldn't decide if I was relieved or disappointed. "You're right," he said. Two words I imagined were difficult for Zavier to utter. "I don't have magic. I'm not a witch, but I was raised by someone who was. Not a blood relative. She was closer to me than my own mother, though."

Several feelings rushed me at once. Pain and sorrow were on the top of the heap. I wasn't the only one opening up. There was a lot he wasn't telling me, but I was beginning to trust the warden. "She's gone, isn't she?" I could see his sadness, feel his pain. It was as real as mine, and it clogged the air between us, reflecting in those starlight eyes.

Tipping back his head, he let out a weary sigh. "It's been two years now, but it feels like yesterday."

Were Zavier and I having a heart-to-heart? I hadn't thought to feel sympathy for the cocky warden, but I guessed it was possible we had more in common than I thought. "The missing them never goes away, does it?" I asked.

"I understand your desire to make the one who took your mother pay, but know it is a dangerous game you're playing. If Lilith is somehow involved, you're in more trouble than I thought."

"How is it you know so much about my life and what I want? Better yet, how do you know about Lilith?"

"The vampire and I have crossed paths a time or two. Neither of us came away without a scar. She isn't someone I would trample with alone. Lilith doesn't have an honest or truthful bone in her body."

"And you do?" I challenged. He wasn't telling me anything I didn't already know.

"I might be willing to color out of the lines, but I know the difference between good and evil."

I hoped so, because there would come a time I might very well need Zavier to save my ass. I thought it best not to mention that yet.

⚜

Zavier and I walked the narrow, pebbled streets of the market with its sunbaked shops. Dusk gave the air a quiet blue hue with hints of lavender. Breathing in the sea, I let the noise of the village drown out the voices in my head.

The past touched every part of my life, so I took the few

moments of calmness, because a storm was on the horizon. I sensed it in the air. Darkness was brewing.

The smear of black rolled in with the fog, so thick it clogged my windpipe. *How does no one else feel it?*

No one else but Zavier Cross, anyway.

Very few wardens were open to things such as prophesies and premonitions, yet Zavier took everything I threw at him in stride. The man was definitely not human, and the more I pondered on it, the more certain I was. My instincts were telling me he was hiding something, and he was going to great lengths to keep it buried.

"Colin is concerned that you are up to no good," Zavier said, breaking the silence.

As he should be. "What do you plan to tell him?" I asked. Zavier knew my secrets. He knew about the coven meetings, that Lilith was looking for a witch, most likely me, and that I hadn't given up my desire for revenge, but I knew none of Zavier's secrets. He had an unfair advantage, but not for long. I'd find a way to uncover the truth, and if there was one thing I was, it was persistent, annoyingly so.

His brows furrowed. "I haven't decided. I guess it depends on you, and if you plan to continue this absurd notion to kill Lilith."

The patter of our footsteps sounded in time. "If I told you I no longer wished to see her burn, would you believe me?"

"No." he said without hesitation.

"So you don't want me to lie to you?"

"You're not going to reconsider, are you? What if I threaten to tell Colin? Will you give it up then?"

I shook my head. "I don't have a choice. I must. It has gone beyond mere revenge. This is the only way to keep the Bay safe."

"Even if it means your death?" he challenged, as if death would scare me.

"You wouldn't let that happen. I'm counting on your superb skills to keep me alive."

"Skylar, you have a way of making my job very difficult."

I grinned. "I'm keeping you on your toes, comrade."

His lips moved into a frown. "Nobody lives forever, but it is your choice what to do with your future, to go forward or back."

"If I don't have justice, I don't think I'll ever find peace." What was it about Zavier that made me tell him things I'd only ever thought?

He raised a dark brow. "Not even for love?"

I bit my lower lip. "I don't know. I've never been in love."

"Now that's a damn shame." There was humor in his voice.

"And what do you know about love?" Zavier didn't strike me as the kind of guy who was into serious relationships. I hadn't thought of it before, but did he have a girlfriend? The idea made my stomach drop, and there might have been a tinge of jealousy. "Let me guess, girls everywhere fall at your feet."

A grin split his lips. "Well yes, but that's not the point. You broke things off with Liam before it got serious. I'm just saying that revenge can consume you if you let it. You never know what you might be missing out on. Love is like breathing. Once you find it, you can't survive without it."

I rolled my eyes. He sounded like a poet. "Thanks for the pep talk, but my love life is not your concern." I turned the handle on the door to the shop, intending to push it open, but Zavier beat me to it. I gave him a look.

"You look like crap today." Tulip said the moment I strolled in with my shadow behind me.

"Why does everyone keep saying that?" I grumbled.

A faint smile curved on Zavier's lips.

I scowled, suppressing the need to put my elbow into his gut.

Tulip's eyes bounced between the warden and me, and her mouth twitched. "You two are acting weird. So tell me, Zavier, did Sky have a rough night?"

The insinuation in her tone made my cheeks burn. "Tulip," I hissed. "We have work to do," I gritted between my teeth. I went to the counter and unloaded the bag of herbs I had drying from the other day.

Tulip's tawny eyes glanced to the window. "It's raining out in case you hadn't noticed, and I'd much rather interrogate your sexy warden."

What? It was raining? I had been outside a moment ago. When did that happen? My gaze flicked to the window, which was being pummeled with big drops of water. What a strange day this was turning out to be. "Zavier has better things to do than gossip with you."

He cleared his throat.

I was about to tell Zavier to stop encouraging Tulip when the door to the shop blew open, letting in a gust of air and the scent of trouble. Papers whooshed off my desk, scattering on the floor. Two seconds later, Abbey stormed inside, crowding the small space. Her cloak was drenched from the rain, the hood shielding her face, but I could tell something was wrong. Tears mixed with the droplets of water, her eyes puffy and red.

Outside of the coven, the five of us rarely spoke. It was safer that way. If Abbey was here, something was very wrong.

Zavier straightened, his eyes going bright.

"Abbey, what is it? What happened?" I asked.

CHAPTER 11

"It's Katie. She's gone. Ohmygod. What do I do? She's just gone." Abbey started rambling, her words jumbled and not making any sense as she paced from one wall to the other.

I stood and grabbed her hands, forcing her to stop moving and look at me. "Whoa, Abbey. Slow down."

Her face was so pale. I was afraid she might collapse before I understood what had her in such a frantic state. "They took her. The Berkano vampires took my sister."

My equilibrium wavered. Katie? She was a little girl, only eight or nine. What did the vampires want with her? There were rules in place, but as of late, more and more of the laws were being disregarded. "When?" I asked, the wheels in my head spinning.

Tulip looked confused. She knew of the coven, but only knew them by name, had never seen their faces. And here was one trembling, eyes wide, on the brink of hysteria.

Zavier was suddenly beside Abbey, his arm slipped over her shoulder, keeping her on her feet. The muscle in his jaw drummed. I thanked him silently with my eyes, regardless that he was amped up to kick some vampire ass. His anger was outlined in every part of his body, but it was his eyes that shimmered with barely controlled rage. I could taste it in the air.

Abbey's shoulders heaved as a sob tore through her chest. "Y-yesterday."

"Colin said there was an attack yesterday in the village," I prodded.

Abbey nodded. "She was there with my father. What am I going to do?"

I took her hand. "Nothing. You are going to go home and comfort your ma. Colin will handle it. He will get Katie back." I made my voice steady and full of conviction. She had to believe my brother would fix this.

We both needed to believe it. The alternative was too dreadful. If Katie was taken for what I suspected, then the entire coven was at risk.

"I'm afraid, Skylar. This is my fault. If I hadn't—"

"Shh." I wrapped my arms around her. "It's going to be okay."

"I've should have seen this coming," she whispered, holding onto me.

"You know the gift doesn't work that way. We can't always dictate what we see."

"She's just a kid, and I swear, Sky, I can sense her fear. She's so scared and alone."

I pulled back, keeping my hands on her shoulders. "Tulip, can you take Abbey home? Make sure she gets there. We're closing the shop. I need to see Colin."

"You'll be okay?" Tulip asked, already on her feet.

"I've got him," I said, nodding my head at Zavier. He had

remained silent during my exchange with Abbey, but his eyes were as hard as steel.

"Right. You owe me," Tulip muttered as she steered Abbey toward the door. "You know I don't like getting mixed up in your hocus pocus."

She didn't, but my love life she had no problem butting right in. "Take her straight home. Don't talk to anyone."

"In this weather, I wouldn't think about it." And then they were gone, the sheets of rain washing away their outline.

Zavier held the door open as his eyes found mine. "Move your pretty little butt, minx. We need to notify your brother. The longer the vampires have her, the harder it will be to track them and where they've taken her."

He wasn't telling me anything I didn't already know, and I wasn't in the mood to be bossed around. I only wanted to get Katie back, and get rid of the vampire who threatened the entire Bay. "Real helpful," I muttered, intertwining our hands.

A dark brow lifted. "Now might not be the best time to hold hands."

I shot him a hateful look. "Shut up and be quiet. The sound of your voice is breaking my concentration." I squeezed my eyes closed, letting my power seep into my veins. Tingles spread over my body from head to toe, and the rune on my back radiated. Zavier was in for a surprise, and if it had been another situation, I would have enjoyed the look on his face.

Those dark brows furrowed. "What are you—?"

Swoop.

The air surrounding us kicked up in ribbons of magic, and my body became weightless. I tightened my hold on Zavier, letting the spell take us away as we flew into the dark.

When the light broke through the blackness, we were no longer in the shop, but outside, only feet away from the compound. I shrugged as Zavier blinked, pinning me with a stern glare of displeasure. "This was faster," I told him.

"Next time you decide to use your sorcery on me, a little forewarning would be nice," he grumbled, pulling his hand from my clutch and shaking it out.

"I can't make any promises."

Neither of us spoke as we raced up the hill toward the compound. Everyone was going about their business, unaware I was filled with a smorgasbord of emotions. Rage. Worry. Sadness. Outrage.

I was lost in my own head when my name roared from Zavier's lips. Before I could react, he shoved me down. The guards stationed on the ground moved into action, shouting out commands. Through the chaos, Zavier let a steady curse. I glanced at the warden and gasped. Zavier's warm blood was on my hand, and there was an arrow sticking out of his chest.

"Oh my God. You're shot."

"I'll be fine. It missed the heart," he said through gritted teeth. "Are you hurt?" he asked. Pain etched on his face, yet he was concerned about me.

I pushed away from him, to look at how bad the wound was. "Don't move. Let me look at it."

He didn't listen. The next thing I knew, he yanked the arrow out and more blood was flowing.

"Holy fucking hell."

"I bet that hurt. It's what you get for not listening to me," I stated briskly. "Help me get him inside," I instructed the guards closest.

"I don't need their damn help. I can bloody well stand on my own."

Someone was ultra-crabby when in pain. I filed that away for the future if Zavier ever decided to take an arrow for me again. "Fine, but if you bleed out before I get a chance to save you, I'm going to be pissed."

His eyes were like flints of steel, face lined with determination as he pushed to his feet. "This isn't the first time I've been shot, minx, and probably not the last. Your worry for me is touching."

I rolled my eyes.

❧

Colin burst through the door. "How's he doing?"

Rubbing my hands on my thighs, I stood up from where I'd sat on Zavier's bed. "He's angry and uncooperative, but he'll live."

"I'd be more pleasant, if she would stop poking me," Zavier growled.

"I'm grateful for your reflexes, and for keeping my sister safe. I owe you," Colin told the grumpy patient.

"I should have reacted sooner. I won't make that mistake again. Did you find out who it was?"

Colin nodded. "A vampire."

Zavier's head fell back against the pillow, his eyes staring at the ceiling. "Of course it was. He knew I would intercept the arrow."

"Those were my thoughts as well," Colin agreed.

"Why would the vampire try to kill you?" I asked. There was something they weren't saying, and I wanted to know what it was, seeing as they felt the need to keep it from me.

Amusement flickered briefly in Zavier's eyes. "To get to you. The vampire wasn't trying to kill you. He wanted to capture you. Easiest way to do that is to take me out."

I swallowed the golf ball-sized lump that had suddenly

formed in my throat, fighting the urge to sit down again. "She's been searching for a witch with the blood of an original," I said, almost in a trance. Lilith had found me.

"How could she possibly have uncovered the truth about who you are?" Colin wanted to know.

My gaze shifted to Zavier's. I wasn't ready to tell Colin about the coven or the dreams of Lilith. He would only stress out and tighten my security, which would hinder my ability to track the vampire queen. I needed to get a step ahead, instead of always falling two steps behind. "Apparently the secret is out of the bag. She knows I'm a witch."

"It's more than that. She is targeting those with ties to the Rift witches."

Shit. I'd completely forgotten about Katie. All this business of Zavier being hurt, the whole reason for coming back to the compound had escaped my mind. "Colin, during the attack on the village last night, the Berkanos took Abbey's little sister. She is only a child."

"You're sure?" he asked, deep lines of concern etching over his forehead. Colin was a protector at heart. He would do everything in his power to find the girl, even if it meant using *other* means.

"Positive. Abbey came by the shop today in a panic."

Accusation swam in his eyes. "You're still meeting with those witches."

Colin might not approve of magic, but he made it a point to know the people who lived in the Bay, and that included those who were witches and their descendants. If there was trouble that stunk of magic, Colin knew whose door to knock on first. "That is beyond the point, brother. We must find her and get her back before it is too late." Katie was a witch, but a very young one…and impressionable. It was vital she not end up under Lilith's influence.

He nodded. "Of course. You're right. I will send a group to the caves."

Zavier groaned. The idiot had tried to sit up.

I rolled my eyes and pushed at his shoulder lightly, forcing him to lie back down. "You've lost a considerable amount of blood. You need to rest. He's done talking, Colin."

Colin stood over my shoulder, staring at the stubborn man. "I've stationed another warden at your door for the night."

Zavier gave Colin a nod of approval. "I'll be fine by morning."

My jaw hit the ground. "By morning? Are you insane? An arrow pierced your flesh, barely missing your heart, and you think you'll be hunky-dory after a good night's sleep?"

"That drink you forced down my throat was a toxin, wasn't it?" Zavier inquired.

"Yes, but—"

Colin placed a hand on my shoulder. "Let him be, Sky. He isn't going to heal any faster with you hounding him."

"Now the two of you are ganging up on me. Since you seem to know what is best for yourself, I guess I'm no longer needed." I spun around, my hair whipping in the air.

"Minx, there's no need to get your feathers ruffled."

My scowled deepened as I paused and glared over my shoulder.

Minx? my brother mouthed.

I sighed. "The toxin must be working. He should be asleep in a minute."

"You drugged me?" Zavier's words began to slur like one of the burly patrons at the pub. "I told you she was a minx."

I frowned as his eyes fluttered close. "He should be out for the night, resting as his body needs. Make sure no one disturbs him."

Colin crossed his arms, his feet planted apart in a warrior's stance. There was a hint of amusement tugging at the corner of his lips. "Minx, huh? Clever nickname. It suits you."

"If you tell him you said so, I'll make sure there are no children in your future. This friend of yours is quite the nuisance."

"You haven't figured him out yet, have you? It must be killing you."

My eyes narrowed. "What do you know about Zavier?"

"I know he did his job today. He saved you, and I will be eternally grateful. You're all the family I have left, Skylar."

Family. "What happened to the vampire who shot Zavier?"

"He was beheaded."

My chin rose. "Good." I wished I had been the one to sever his head.

Colin must have seen the fleck of satisfaction in my eyes. He placed a gentle hand on my shoulder. "You have to give up this notion of revenge. Do you not see the danger you put yourself in? Look what happened today. This is only the beginning."

"I know, but I refuse to cower at her feet. She will die. I swear it."

He shook his head. "In a way, I pity her, for the day she meets you face to face, it will be her last. I know it. Maybe even she knows it. You're not a witch to be trifled with, but promise me you won't do anything stupid. I can't lose you, too."

"Have you met me? I wouldn't be me if I didn't act before thinking, but I will promise you I won't ditch my warden if that makes you feel better. He's kind of growing on me." I looked over my shoulder at Zavier. In sleep, the hardness of his face softened, making him appear tender.

Colin exhaled. "I can't decide if that is a good thing or not, but I'll take the small victory."

❧

THERE WERE faces in the fire—warriors, vampires, and witches. And in the flames were battles of courage and death. Of triumphs and loss. Love and sacrifice—and all that came with war between dark and light.

I stared at the faces, letting the golden glow of the dancing flames warm my clammy skin. Each day, the threat of Lilith closed in on me. There was only so much I could handle in twenty-four hours, and after seeing Zavier's blood on my hands and knowing Katie was still missing, my body and mind were exhausted.

Phones and convenient communication was a thing of the past. I had thought the coven might reach out once word spread about Abbey's sister, but the only faces in the hearth tonight were those of the past.

I didn't want to be alone, but solitude was exactly what I was getting this night. Liam was avoiding me like the plague, and Colin was off with the group of guards who had set forth to the vampire's known nest. God knew how many more we didn't know about, and it was doing me no good sitting here, nibbling on my nails worrying about them.

Leaving the curtain and the window open, I allowed in the night and began to drift off as I listened to the sounds of crickets, the rustling of leaves, and the gentle lull of the surf.

The knock on the door brought me out of the half sleep and into mild annoyance. Rolling out of bed, I padded across the room and threw open the door.

"Zavier?"

CHAPTER 12

I blinked more than once. "What are you doing out of bed?"

He stood in the doorway, his body shadowed in darkness, except for the dwindling firelight catching the glint of his eyes. "I wanted to thank you."

My fingers ran through my hair. "Right now? You could have done so in the morning." I angled my head to the side. "Why aren't you sleeping?" I forced my eyes to stay on his face. Where was his shirt?

Right. I had cut it off to tend to the wound, so in a roundabout why, it was partially my fault he was standing in my doorway nearly naked.

A slow grin curved on his lips as sharp silver eyes took my measure. "The toxin must have been weak."

I was in nothing but my favorite T-shirt. I tugged on the hem, which barely covered my ass, and after those glittering eyes had taken their fill, I felt exposed and feverish. "Not likely," I mumbled, pushing at my hair again. How had he gotten so close?

Zavier leaned forward, the side of his cheek rubbing against mine as the stubble of his day-old beard tickled my skin. "You smell like orange blossoms."

And he smelled like trouble.

Nerves I didn't know I had frayed as I reached behind me for the handle. "You should go back to bed."

"Not yet." He crossed to me, laying his hands on either side of the wooden door.

My eyes stayed on his, following his movements. "If you've ripped open what I've mended, I'll shoot you with an arrow myself." My fingers went to check under the bandage, but got hung up on his stomach, sliding over hard abs. He was built like Adonis, a freaking God. His breath hissed, and muscle trembled as my fingers grazed his flesh, light as a butterfly's wing. I was drawn to his face, captured by the intense shimmer of silver that caused my heart to skip.

It took more effort than I would admit to drag my eyes back to his chest. Not that staring at his toned golden skin was less intoxicating. My hands slid over the cotton wrap still secured to his torso, and I peeled back a corner, expecting to see fresh blood. I tried not to think about the fact I was touching him, or how incredible it felt.

I'd make good on my threat if he reopened the wound. It had taken all my strength to calm the rattled storm within me to steady my hand so I could mend him. Something had happened to me when I caught sight of Zavier hurt. It scared me on a level I never wanted to feel again, and now, being this close to him, made me all kinds of scattered.

Concentrate on checking the wound.

And I did just that, peeling away the bandage to reveal… My gaze snapped upward. "It's healed."

"I told you I'd be fine."

I ran my finger over the slightly pinkish spot that only hours ago I'd sewn shut. "How can that be?"

He gave a lazy one-shoulder shrug. "Asks the girl who traveled from one spot to another with nothing but a bat of her lashes."

"Bullshit. I have a valid reason. Magic. I'm a witch. What the hell is yours?"

"You have your talents, and I have mine."

My hand grabbed the edge of the door. "If you aren't going to give me a straight answer, then you can get out."

He put his foot out, stopping the door from closing in his face. "You don't want to be alone. I'm here."

I chewed on the inside of my lip. These abilities Zavier had were troublesome, like the man himself, but he was right. I didn't want to be alone. There was something evil in the night —lurking, stalking, waiting—and I knew when I fell into sleep, she would be waiting for me there. "This is a bad idea," I whispered, fighting the urge to latch my fingers onto his chest.

He cocked a brow. "And your point is?"

"I don't know anymore."

"You like me."

True. It never stopped me from making bad decisions before...but Zavier was different. Why? I wasn't sure. "What part of this expression makes you think that?" I asked, drawing an air circle around my face.

His fingers ran down my arms, sending tendrils of warmth over my skin. "If I don't affect you, I'm curious what does." He took me with both hands, a quick jerk that slammed my body to his.

"Zavier." His name tumbled from my lips in a shaky sigh.

"Nervous, are you?"

I stayed where I was, my gaze never wavering from his smoldering look. "Isn't that what you want?"

The air around us suddenly lashed and swirled, extinguishing the fire in the hearth. "You should be nervous. Probably a little afraid, too, of just what I'm capable of. If you hadn't kissed me… If I didn't know what you taste like… I might be able to get you out of my head."

I tipped my chin up. "I'm not scared of you, and you won't hurt me."

"I guess we'll see." He took my mouth, hard and fast, trapping me against the door with his glorious body as his hands laced with mine.

Everything inside me ebbed and flowed like the ocean tide. The muscles of his back and shoulders rippled under my fingertips as they dug into his skin. I wanted to touch so much more of him, and that worried me.

"I won't hurt you," he groaned, lowering his voice as he ran his nose down my neck. "I could never hurt you." Then his lips were assaulting mine again, stealing both breath and will.

Backing me into the room, he kicked the door behind him and we were plunged into darkness.

I shivered.

He grabbed my backside, hoisting me up against the wall, and shoved his body to the length of mine. Gasping, I arched, offering myself as my fingers combed gently through his midnight hair. It felt as if my body was meant for his, and if I believed in a thing such as soul mates, I might have believed Zavier was mine.

A hunger built between us, beyond sanity. His mouth was sweet, so sweet on mine, our tongues dancing and teasing. My spirit soared, my mind sighed, and my heart melted for him, for his touch.

"You better hold on," he murmured.

I let out a quick cry of alarm as he swooped me up. Then I was flying through the dark before I found myself under him on the bed, his fingers tugging up my shirt. In seconds, we were flesh to flesh.

"I can't think," I murmured.

"Good. I must be doing something right." His mouth silenced any other protest.

Not that I was complaining. How could I when his hands were all over my body, driving me to a crest of pleasure so intense I had to scream?

His lips captured my sounds of desire, my body straining beneath his. He knew what I was reaching for, what I was burning up for. I swore the man could read my mind, knew what I wanted before the thought entered my head. It was a dangerous and sensual gift.

My head fell back. I wanted quick, fiery passion, but he switched gears on me, savoring every curve and swell of my body with skilled hands. I hadn't known I had so many undiscovered sensitive spots. Maybe it was just Zavier's touch that made it so.

He gripped my wrists in his hand, pulling my arms over my head. I had long since surrendered myself to Zavier's mercy. I'd never wanted anyone, anything, the way I desired him in this moment. I lost control over what was happening to me the second he slid exquisitely inside me with such thick heat.

Everything escalated. Damp strands of hair plastered to my neck and shoulders. My lower body exploded with bliss, a sensation so overwhelming I craved more. In wonder, my eyes flew open and my breath froze. I held onto him, fingers tightening as the shudders wracked through me.

I cried out, at least I thought I did; I wasn't sure of anything anymore. His mouth reclaimed mine, and he thrust one more time to join me in sweet ecstasy, my name a murmur against my lips.

※

WHAT HAD I DONE? Oh God. I just had mind-blowing, body-humming sex without a single thought about the consequences. I hadn't thought at all, only felt, and that was the problem.

He made me lose myself, lose my control, and it scared me. Our bodies had melted together like liquid heat, making me feel things I shouldn't have felt, didn't want to feel. He was still inside me, and I had to fight the urge to wrap my legs around him and sink deeper with way more willpower than I was comfortable with.

The thought of the splendid pleasure even the slightly movement would bring brought a moan to the tip of my tongue. I closed my eyes, bit my lip, and forced myself to swallow the sound. I might not have been able to stop what had already happened, but I could prevent myself from making the mistake again.

I opened my mouth and he moved. Damn him.

He gathered me close, his lips brushing over my hair as I wrestled with myself. My brain told me not to spend the night with him, that it was just sex, but my heart wanted him to stay, wanted to be held. Being in his arms engulfed me with a sense of security I hadn't known I longed for. The world outside my bedroom was harsh and unpredictable, but in this little room with Zavier, I wanted to let go of my anger and hatred, let in emotions I'd long ago locked away in.

Zavier brushed the damp strands of hair off my face. "Do you use magic to enhance your appearance? I swear, sometimes when I look at you, it's like you're changing right in front of my eyes. How can your already-staggering beauty possibly increase?"

Wow. He was going to make the whole business of kicking him out of my bed difficult. I never imagined the dark warden was capable of sweet words. Be still my beating heart. "Do you use that line on every witch you sleep with?" I tried to keep my tone light, refusing to let much his words had moved me show.

He lifted those hooded eyes. "Nah, just the ones with bewitching eyes."

Good lord. What had this man done to my body? If I wasn't careful, I could lose more than my head around him, and I wasn't ready to let my heart get tangled with anyone yet. "It's getting late…" I started, but the words felt like sandpaper in my throat.

"I'm not leaving, Skylar. So stop the internal battle and close your eyes. You need to sleep."

I sighed. "How the hell can you always know what I'm feeling?"

"You weren't complaining a few minutes ago," he pointed out.

"I guess it has it benefits, but I'm thinking they might not outweigh all the other hours in the day when I don't want you in my head."

He leaned forward near my ear and whispered, "Do you care to wager I can change your mind?"

To answer his seductive question, I closed my eyes and curled into his arms, forcing my body to relax.

His chest rumbled under my cheek. "That's what I thought."

Considering the day I had, it was no surprise I drifted to sleep moments after my eyes fluttered shut. And with it came the very thing I wanted to avoid.

The dream took me under, and in the darkness, someone called my name.

Abbey?

My heart sank.

A woman with obsidian, choppy hair came into focus. Her face was one I knew well, but wished I had never laid eyes on. Today more than ever, I longed to be able to reach through the barrier of dreams and harm her. Blood for blood. I wanted her to suffer for the pain she had caused me, and continued to cause in the Bay.

In my head, I railed at her, screaming for her to release Katie and take me instead. If she needed a prisoner, I would have gladly stepped in her place.

Lilith glided down the dark and damp corridor to what had to be a chamber. She was underground, another vampires with her. Long tunnels forked off in multiple directions, chamber after chamber lining both sides of the hall, and a chill tiptoed down my spine as I wondered how many people she had locked down there.

In the caves, she had fashioned herself a palace, undoubtedly thinking she deserved no less. The light of the torches sparkled off the gold and silver she draped her body with. All the jewels in the world didn't make her worthy of a throne. However much she desired to rule.

Over my dead corpse.

Destroying Division Fourteen to gain her power back

meant little to her, as did the lives she took. What a fool. Without Frisco Bay, there'd be no land, no life, no blood.

The metal door of one of the chambers shrilled open, followed by a whimper in the dark. A smile donned on her lips when Lilith shined the torch in her hand inside. The light cast flickering shadows into the room and over the damp ceiling.

I gasped, unable to believe what I was seeing. This couldn't be real. It had to be someone messing with my head—another witch—one Lilith had power over. My eyes didn't want to consider what they were seeing.

Abbey was shackled, her hands and feet bound in chains. Tears fell down her cheeks as she glanced up into a pair of sultry blue eyes shining in the dark.

My head shook back and forth, my own tears stinging my eyes. I called out her name, but it was useless, for this was only a dream.

But as the thought flittered through my brain, I was positive Lilith had managed to capture my friend—a witch who was part of my coven. My guess, Abbey was there to save her sister. She'd been the bait, and Abbey had fallen into the dark queen's net.

The vampire beside Lilith flashed to a cowering Abbey and hauled her to her feet. "Maybe you'd like to play a little game of chase?" The vampire laughed at his sadistic joke, a wild and demented sound.

I wanted to carve his soulless eyes out with a hot poker and yank his bloodsucking fangs out by the roots so they'd never grow back. *Prick*. He had just earned himself a place on my hit list.

"I'll even give you a head start, little witch," he hissed in her ear, eagerness dilating his pupils.

Regardless of the fear in Abbey's wide gaze, she tilted her chin up. "Fuck off." Then she spit in the bastard's face.

That's my girl. Pride swelled within me. She wasn't going to go down without a fight, despite the fact she was ten different kinds of scared shitless. It came off her in waves. I could feel it vibrating inside me, amplifying my own fear.

We both knew there would be consequences for such bold actions. The vampire backhanded her, sending Abbey to the ground.

Lilith entered the chamber, tsking her tongue. "Now, Silas, that isn't how we treat our guests." She wore black robes edged in red. Her hair was thick, framing her face in dark slashes. "Abbey." She gestured toward my friend with a sweeping of an arm. "How about we have ourselves a little girl chat?"

Abbey only whimpered.

Lilith leaned near her ear, whispering something beyond my hearing. Then the vampire queen straightened, the smile on her lips too full of mischief and self-pleasure.

With a rustle of her silk dress, Lilith spun around, turning her back to the witch huddled in the corner. Abbey's shoulders quaked from tears. I wanted to comfort her, to let her know she wasn't alone, that I would find her, but the dream was a barrier I couldn't penetrate.

Lilith lifted an ornate item she had been holding—a mirror. She stared at her reflection in the glass, but instead of the beautiful temptress, an older woman whose skin was weathered, drooping into folds, showed. Her obsidian hair was thin and gray. The mirror showed her aging years, decades, centuries. A vampire's life might have once been eternal, but the Rift had changed all of that.

On a scream of rage, Lilith hurled the mirror, smashing

glass over the cavern floor. Storming to Abbey, Lilith yanked back the witch's head, extended her fangs, and struck, tearing into her ivory throat with voraciousness. She drank fast and deep, until the light in Abbey's eyes went blank.

I screamed.

CHAPTER 13

I woke sitting straight up, screaming, icy terror hitting me in the gut, but not for me.

Oh, Abbey. Not Abbey.

Zavier's arms curled around me, soothing me until I could get control of the sobs racking through my body. "Hey. It's okay. You're okay. It was only a dream."

No! No! No!

It wasn't only a dream. I buried my face into his chest, holding on as if my life depended on it...and in a way, it did. I tried to tell him it had been a vision, that Lilith had wanted me to see, to know she was getting closer, but tears and pain made it impossible to speak.

"What happened? What did you see?" His fingers stroked my hair.

"Oh God. I couldn't..." To my horror, my voice wavered as my eyes filled with tears again, my insides churned up. "S-she killed her."

Zavier's eyes narrowed, slanting like a cat's. "Who? Lilith?"

My fingers curled into fists, my body tense. "Abbey," I whispered hoarsely. "The vampire queen killed her. I saw it."

"You're sure?"

"For someone who is always so perceptive, you question me now?"

He gave a curt nod. "We need to tell Colin."

"I don't know if he is even back yet. What if it was a trap?" The idea of my brother getting hurt or captured sent me into a tizzy. There was another emotional break building inside me, and it was right on the horizon. I needed to keep it together, but it wasn't as easy as a snap of my fingers.

The hints of blue in his irises gleamed with heat. "We'll get word to your brother."

This was one of those times I wished cell phones were still a thing. My eyes were wet, the lashes sticking together. "I should have known. I should have protected her." Abbey was part of the coven because of me. It had been my idea. I was the one who had recruited them.

Zavier hooked a finger under my chin, forcing me to look at him. "Hey. This isn't your fault."

I disagreed, but it would be pointless to argue. "Crying pisses me off."

"I know," he murmured. "Better to let it out now. I swear you'll feel better."

"I'll get it together in a minute," I said after an ugly sniffle that suggested I was going to need more than a minute. "Do you have a sister or something?" He was awfully good with this whole consoling thing. It made my attraction to him increase a notch for some stupid reason.

"No. But I do have one annoying, pain-in-the-ass brother."

"Wow. We have something in common. Who would have thought?"

Zavier brushed the hair off my face. "You okay now?"

"No," I said honestly. "But I'm going to make that bitch pay for what she's done." *She would suffer first. I swear it. Another vow I intend to keep.* Anger snapped inside me, like little bolts of lightning.

He held out his hand. "What are we waiting for?"

I lifted my head, regarding Zavier. He was so different from any warden I knew. Liam never would have encouraged my deep desire for revenge, let alone want to help. I might learn to like the jerk. Zavier was turning out to be quite useful, and not just in bed.

With a stiff lip, I set those feelings of utter sadness and loss aside, concentrating on the fury pulsing within me. I placed my hand in his.

He gave my fingers a squeeze.

As I moved to the edge of the bed, a dog howled through the open window. My whole body locked up.

It was a sound I knew well, one that had often haunted my dreams as a child. *Her hounds. Lilith's devilish pets.*

"They're coming," I whispered.

"Who is?" Zavier asked.

I dragged my gaze from the moonlit terrace, turning toward Zavier. His eyes were glowing. "Get up. Get dressed. We don't have much time." My hand flicked out to bring in more light. The hearth roared to life.

Running a hand through his disheveled hair, Zavier caught the pants I threw at him. "You could at least tell me who or what is coming."

"Her dogs. Hurry. Can't you hear them howling?" I moved around the room, tossing random clothes on.

Zavier tugged on his pants, and then gave me a weird look. "No. I don't hear anything."

"I'm telling you, she's let them loose. They're hunting. We have to do something. We have to stop them." No one else was going to die tonight. Not if I could do something to stop it. I hadn't been able to help Abbey, and I had no idea if Katie was still alive, but I refused to let Lilith terrorize another soul. And no one better stand in my way.

"I'll alert the wardens who stayed behind," Zavier said as he slipped into his pants.

Finally. Less talk. More action. I threw on my boots and went to the door, expecting him to be right behind me. Outside, the echo of what sounded like a dozen hounds howled, a long, deep warning. "What's taking you so long?" I griped, ready to walk out the door without him.

"I need a shirt. If you remember, someone ripped the one I was wearing after I got shot. Don't move." He used the adjoining door.

I rolled my eyes.

Ten seconds later, he returned with a shirt and blade. "You got a weapon, minx?"

"I don't wear these boots for a fashion statement."

"Good to know."

We headed straight for the warden quarters on the first floor. I didn't even think about what time it was. The guards worked in shifts, but with Colin gone and taking a group, the compound was thin on defense.

Something told me the wicked witch had known, and used it to her advantage, striking when we were at our weakest.

"Has my brother returned?" I asked Doyle, the second in command when Colin wasn't in attendance.

"Not yet," the older warden said. His temples were peppered with silver strands.

"We're about to get some unexpected company. How many wardens are in the compound?" Zavier demanded.

"Ten, maybe fifteen," Doyle replied.

I groaned. "It will have to do. The compound is about to be under attack. Get everyone you can."

Doyle straightened his shoulders. "Are you certain?"

Zavier slammed his hands down on the desk. "Did she stutter? Unless you want to explain to Colin how his sister wound up in the clutches of the Berkano vampires, I'd move your ass."

"What's going on?" a fourth voice came from around the corner.

I spun and sighed. "Liam. Thank God. There's no time to explain, but Lilith has released her hounds."

Liam's gaze went over my head, waves of testosterone pouring off him. This was the first time Liam and I had spoken since the night I had ended things. Something told me he wasn't as happy to see me as I was to see him. "You're sleeping with him," Liam shouted.

I didn't understand what that had to do with what I had told him, or why he wasn't barking orders. "Did you hear what I said?" Now was not the time to make a spectacle and air our dirty laundry, but he seemed dead set on doing just that. "Or have you conveniently forgotten what happened the last time her hounds were set loose?"

Doyle shifted on his feet, looking about as uncomfortable as I was starting to feel. Today was not the day to mess with my emotions.

A grim line set on Liam's lips. "I'm having a tough time believing anything that comes out of your mouth."

Great. Nothing like being called a liar in front of everyone.

Zavier stepped in between Liam and me, and shoved Liam

in the chest. "Back off. What she does in her personal life isn't your concern anymore. You *should* be concerned with the pack of hellhounds barking at our gates. It is only a matter of time before they break in. And we both know what they are looking for."

All eyes turned to me. I blanched and then flushed.

"You better not be wrong about this," Liam seethed.

Tension between the two wardens rippled in the air as they stared each other, neither backing down. "Colin trusts me, and deep down, you and I want the same thing."

The stare down continued, and the lack of production was making me antsy. Liam finally gave a curt nod before sounding the alarm.

"Was that necessary?" I muttered.

"It got the job done. Besides, he was wasting time that could be spent gathering what little defense we have."

No argument there. When it came to intimidation, Zavier seemed to have a knack for it.

Together, we moved down the long corridors, through the great hall, and into the night.

"Stay close to me," he advised, his gaze meeting mine.

I scanned the night, over the sea and into the woods. "I don't see anything yet. What if I'm wrong?"

The wind blew in, carrying the scent of death, foul and ugly. Zavier uncoiled his arms and pushed up his sleeves, flashing the sword in his clutches. "You're not. I can sense them."

"Then what is taking the assholes so long?"

"You anxious to get the chance to use that knife?"

I glanced at Zavier from the corner of my eye. "If you keep talking, I might be tempted to use it on you."

The wind rose, snapping through the trees and over the

water as feral howls rolled through the air in desperation. Magic surged under my skin, my breath whistling in and out of my lungs as I ordered myself to stay calm. I concentrated on what was to come, forcing my legs to remain planted and firm. I wouldn't run in fear, and ignored the instinct. Abbey's face played through my head, fueling my anger.

The first wave tumbled out of the viscous fog, pouring up the hill with barred teeth and sharp claws. Eyes of blood radiated through the dark.

Zavier's sword sliced in a sharp stroke, cleaving the head of a hound as it lunged. My hand clutched on my blade, the other touched the rune etched into the back of my neck. Fire shot down my arm, engulfing the sleek silver knife.

Zavier arched his brows. "Neat trick. Do me a favor…don't get bit."

"I'm not planning on it."

With a furious growl, a hound streaked toward me, leaping to snag the end of my shirt in its jaws. In a blur of speed, a dark shape flashed out of the shadows. Zavier's sword swept down behind me seconds before fangs sank into my hip.

"Watch your back, minx."

I smirked. "That's what you're for."

He wiped the end of his blade on his thigh. "Oh, now you want my help."

Lilith's hounds could rip limbs using their jaws only—notorious killers, and one was staring me down. Matted, coarse hair covered its body. Rows of serrated teeth shined as the hound peeled back its lips in a growl. The beast wasn't alone. Two others appeared.

Zavier stepped in front of me, twirling his blade in a full circle. "Remember to stay calm. And don't let them get you on the ground."

"This isn't my first rodeo."

The hounds attacked.

I hacked, punched, and pivoted, using my combined skills of fighting and magic, but only pulling out the powerful stuff when necessary. I didn't want to attract any extra unwanted attention my way. I glanced at my warden.

"Zavier!" I shrieked. A hound was shredding his forearm. Blood dripped to the ground. He didn't even flinch.

I made the mistake of taking my eyes off the other hound, and it cost me. A bear-sized paw swiped in the air, catching me in the chin and whipping my head to the side.

"Skylar!" Zavier bellowed.

Fear struck like an arrow vibrating in my chest as the beast leered over me, its fangs dripping slimy goop as it foamed at the mouth.

Disgusting.

Zavier's warning echoed in my head as its massive claws pinned my arms and dug into my flesh. The mutt roared. It was like having Godzilla scream in my face.

I flung my hands up, latching onto the creature's thick muzzle. Light flashed from my fingers, red as blood and hot as a lash from the devil himself. The force of it would have shot me backward if I wasn't already on the ground. The hound wasn't so fortunate. He went sailing through the air.

I stumbled to my feet. Chaos whirled around me in a mad blur of battle and death.

Zavier shot forward, and thank god he was so damn fast. His hands were around the hound's neck in a second. He didn't hesitate, his hands twisting.

The crack was a deafening sound that swallowed the hound's cry.

Zavier's hand slipped along my cheek and into my hair. "Are you okay?"

My heart pounded in my ribcage. I nodded as best as I could. "What took you so long?"

He chuckled. "Just keeping you on your toes."

CHAPTER 14

The moon dipped low in the sky, ribboning the first of its orange fire. I pulled the clip from my hair, and shook out the curls.

Zavier's eyes scanned my body, before he slipped an arm around my waist. "You're bleeding."

My hand went to my face. "It's nothing that won't heal. I've had way worse. Trust me."

He guided me toward the compound. My body ached, but the pain made me happy to be alive. A chilly air caressed my cheek, taking away some of the sting. At the top of the hill stood a figure outside the compound walls, the moonlight blurring their face.

I squinted, and then my heart tripped over. "Colin," I exhaled, my shoulders relaxing for the first time in hours. I took off and threw my arms around his neck. "I was so worried."

Colin let a weary chuckle, his arms slow to wrap around me. "You're okay." He pulled back, eyes sweeping over my face.

I swallowed the knot of emotion. "Just a few scratches. I'm fine."

"You knew she released the hounds?"

I nodded. "We were able to fend them off before they reached the village."

Colin's eyes lifted over my head. "Thank you," he said to Zavier.

The warden gave a slight nod. "If it wasn't for Skylar, the hounds would have had the advantage. She gave us enough time to form a defense."

"Let me guess, she was also barking orders." Colin ruffled the top of my head. "Sometimes I forget how dangerous she can be."

"That I can definitely attest to."

I rolled my eyes, but was too happy to have Colin alive and home to protest. The wardens who had gone with Colin began to shuffle inside the compound, looking like they could all use a shower and ten hours of uninterrupted sleep.

A movement from behind my brother caught my attention. I angled my head to the side for a better view. Five little fingers clutched the end of his shirt, and a head peeked out.

"Katie?" I whispered.

A little girl with big brown eyes stared up at me, half her face shielded behind Colin. She looked afraid to let go of him, and I didn't blame her. My brother was trustworthy and steadfast.

My hands flew to my mouth. "Oh my God, Colin. You found her."

There was a flicker of sadness in his eyes. "Sky, I—"

I shook my head, preventing him from saying anything more in front of Katie. "I already know. I saw it." Tears threatened to spring to my eyes, but I shoved them back, not wanting to alarm the girl any more than she already was. God knew she'd been through an ordeal, and it wasn't over yet. She looked so much like Abbey.

Colin's eyes widened, and then he cautiously encouraged the little girl to his side. "She doesn't understand what's happened."

Crouching, I looked into her frightened face. "Hey, Katie, do you know who I am?"

She clutched onto the back of Colin's shirt, and shook her head. Her lower lip trembled.

I didn't blame her for being wary, and I hadn't expected her to remember me. In truth, kids scared me.

Colin put a hand on top of Katie's head, like he had when I was younger. "Take her inside and get her cleaned up, will you? I'm going to send someone to find her parents."

He was going to break the good and bad news himself. That was the thing with Colin. Regardless that he was bone tired and basically a walking zombie, he would find the last thread of energy to do this deed. It was why he made an exceptional leader.

I looked at Katie, and my mind went blank. What was I supposed to do? Little girls weren't my expertise. I'd been surrounded by warriors and swords growing up, not ribbons and dolls. How old was Katie? Eight? Nine?

Zavier crouched, once again becoming my knight in shining armor. *Careful, Sky, feelings are messy business.*

He held out his hand. "You hungry? I bet we can find something to eat. You like cake?"

Katie's scared eyes sized up the warden, but at the mention of something sweet, she nodded and put her small hand into his.

I walked beside him and the little girl into Silent Bend.

"Smooth, going for bribery, even if it has a creepy-predator-with-a-white-van-to-lure-kids quality," I mumbled.

Zavier leaned in, close to my ear. "You should be one to talk. I'd never seen the deer-caught-in-headlights look from you before. I'm not sure who was more scared, you or the kid."

I shook my head. "So, I'm not great with kids."

"Shocker."

I cracked a smile, pushing open the door to the kitchen.

Getting Katie back felt like a small victory, even though we'd lost Abbey. It was how she would have wanted it. Lilith sought to send a message, and I received it loud and clear, but if it was her intent to make me fear her or get me to be complicit in her ploy, she was sadly mistaken.

My desire to see the vampire queen perish had only intensified. I was coming for her, when she least expected it. I wouldn't give her a fair warning, and those who stood in my way would met the same fate.

৩৯৫

I RAN my shop like I ran my life. With a style born out of instinct, and mostly out of my own personal amusement, but that didn't mean I wasn't a crafty business woman. I enjoyed doing things my way and on my own time.

What bored me, I ignored, and what piqued my interest, I pursued.

And right now, Zavier Cross intrigued me.

Probably too much.

I sipped from a mug, letting the strong coffee smooth my mood. Lilith wanted my coven, wanted *my* power. I was strong with my circle, but I wouldn't let her have what was mine. I would prevail over the bitch, and the last breath she took would be taken by my hand.

"You are right. It is your duty to stop her."

I turned.

A woman stood in the streaming morning sunlight, dust particles swirling around the long dress of dark blue.

It was almost like looking into a mirror; the hair, the eyes, and the shape of the face were identical to mine.

"Mom?" I wanted to run to her, throw my arms around her neck, smell the sweet scent of honeysuckle that always lingered after she left a room, but as I took a step forward, I knew she was an apparition of the past.

Disappointment tornadoed through me. Could I touch her? Would her skin be warm or cold like the dead? I wasn't sure I wanted to find out. The memories of her alive were so much sweeter.

"Aye. You're my blood. My daughter." She touched the amulet that hung at my neck. It had been hers, and I was never without it. "I am of the original witches, but it is you who will have to finish what we set out to do."

"How am I to stop her? She never leaves the safety of her den, and even if I could get inside, the caves and tunnels are crawling with vampires. I'm not sure my coven is strong enough, not now…" My voice trailed off as I thought about Abbey. We were one less member, our power weakened by her loss.

"Love. It is another candle against the darkness. Believe," she whispered, and then she vanished. A shimmer of what looked like a thousand fireflies descended before fizzing out.

I blinked.

Love.

Was she kidding? That was her advice. What did that

mean? The love I had for my coven? For my brother? For a lover? A friend? There were so many forms of love. I wanted to will her back, beg her for help, but I couldn't. Once again, I was on my own and sadness shot through me.

"Who were you talking to?" Zavier asked. He was crouched in front of me, his hands on my knees. Those silver eyes were surprisingly gentle, softening his usually fierce features. "You're eyes, they went blank. You were looking right through me, and no matter how many times I called your name, you stayed as still as a statue."

Tears pricked at my lashes, but with a deep breath, I kept them at bay. "I'm sorry. The vision hit me out of nowhere."

He stood to his full height, the sun slanting at his back and a scowl marring his lips. "Don't ever do that again. How am I to protect you when you go to a place where I can't reach you."

I folded my fingers together, pressing them into my lap as I got myself in control. The vision had left me emotionally raw. "I was in no danger. It was my mother."

The lines on his forehead deepened. "I don't like it, seeing you space out like that."

No, he wouldn't. Magic wasn't something he could control, and that would burn the warden's ass. "I'll try to remember that the next time a spirit summons me from the other side."

He threw me a look of dismay. "This isn't a joke. You aren't safe. Nowhere. If Abbey can be found and taken, so can you. There is nothing Lilith won't do to get her hands on you, even use the dead."

I sighed, taking his hand and lacing our fingers. "I know. My intention was not to alarm you. Believe it or not, I'm trying to save us all."

His expression hardened. "When did it become *your* job to save Frisco Bay? *Alone*?"

"Probably the day my mother died."

Zavier shook his head, eyes skimming out the window, up and down the market. "We shouldn't even be here. Have Tulip run the shop for a few days, until the situation with the vampires is under control. It would be best. You need to be somewhere where you can be protected at all times. The compound."

My back stiffened. "Sounds like you want to lock me in the tower."

"The thought has crossed my mind, but I figured you'd find a way to escape. You always do."

My finger tapped on my leg. "Finally, you're starting to understand me."

"Let's go," he demanded curtly as he leaned down and slipped a hand under my elbow.

I jerked my arm out of his grasp, glowering. "I'm not going anywhere with you."

"Minx, you have two choices, but both end with you tucked away behind the walls of Silent Bend. It's your choice. We can do this the hard way, or you can walk out of here on your own."

Okay. Maybe he hadn't learned enough about me. If he had, he would have known that the caveman approach never worked with me. Nope. Just the opposite. I flicked out both hands, aqua flames dancing over my palms. "I'd like to see you try."

"Temper. Temper," he tsked, and if I wasn't mistaken, there was a hint of a smirk on his lips, as if he was looking forward to the challenge.

Defiance sparked inside me as I stood from my seat. "You can take your ultimatum and shove it up your dead hole."

"Have it your way." Zavier moved with lightning speed. The second he stirred, I let one of the shimmering spheres of light zip through the air. He dipped his shoulder and the ball zoomed past him, hitting the wall. Then he was hoisting me up like a sack of potatoes over his shoulder.

I squealed as I lost my breath, but the second it returned I was going to zap Zavier Cross into Timbuktu. To my frustration, the man moved impossibly quick. He was already strutting across the room. "No magic," he growled, anticipating my retaliation. "Or you'll be sorry."

Like a threat was going to stop me. As I was about to give him the jolt of his life, the door to the shop flew open and Tulip stumbled back.

She stopped in the doorway when she caught sight of Zavier and me. "Oh, sorry, am I interrupting some creepy foreplay you two have?"

Zavier's hand was on my ass. I'd like to think it was there to hold me steady, but I'd bet there was an ulterior motive. "Tulip," I exhaled, blowing a piece of hair out of my face since I still hung upside over Zavier's shoulder. "Will you tell this Neanderthal to put me down?"

Tulip turned her head sideways to get a glimpse of my face. "Um, I don't think I will. My guess is he is probably stopping you from doing something foolish. If so, I support it completely."

"Thank you. I knew we'd get along," Zavier said.

Tulip fanned herself, leaning against the wall. "Dear God. Don't stop talking. Your voice is lethal to the heart."

I couldn't see his face, but I didn't need to. I could tell the fool was grinning.

Tulip's hand covered her heart, and she sighed. "I swear to God, my ovaries just sung."

"You're supposed to be my best friend," I pointed out, irked with the situation. The blood was rushing to my head.

"And as your best friend, I'm telling you I would give my left boob to trade places with you right now."

Zavier chuckled, his body rumbling.

"There's something wrong with both of you," I shot through a curtain of hair.

"Don't worry. I'll take care of the shop," she called as he walked through the door.

That was very generous of her, but it was not the kind of help I was looking for. I pinched Zavier's behind.

"Minx," Zavier roared deep from his chest.

"Argh. You are the most frustrating man. Fine. Take me home, but do it quickly, for I don't know how much longer I can hold myself back."

"There's a first time for everything."

CHAPTER 15

Days turned to weeks, and the attacks in the village grew in numbers. It had the entire Bay on edge, and who could blame them? Lilith was a name feared, and her destruction spread over the land, keeping the people in a constant state of distress.

It had to stop.

Cassidy Harmon breezed into my room like a bolt of sunshine. I did a double take, wondering if I had accidently left my bedroom door open.

"Come on. We need to get you ready," Cassidy said, flipping her golden hair over her shoulder.

My whole body went into shock. "For what?" I snapped. Nothing good ever happened when Cassidy and I were in the same room. I couldn't figure out why my brother wasted his time with her. He was too good for the fake bitch. Not to mention, I had plans. Tonight, I was meeting with the coven. We had much to discuss. The restriction on my movements put me in a sour mood. Colin thought it best I avoided the village until it was safe again. I missed my shop. I missed my life. And there was only one person to blame.

Zavier.

"For the council. You didn't forget, did you?" Cassidy batted her baby blues.

Of course I did. There was about a million other things on my mind than some damn stuffy political soiree. I left all that garbage to my brother. The vampires were up to no good, and the council wanted to throw a freaking party. As if that was going to solve anything, other than their need to drink themselves stupid. "No, I didn't forget. I just don't know why I need to be there."

"It's important," she reminded me in a sweet voice as if she liked me. We both knew the truth, so I didn't see the reason for the charade. If only Colin could look beyond the pretty face. "Colin wants to show the council a united front, that he can continue on what his father started and further build and improve the city."

Blah. Blah. Blah. This was how interested I was in the wheeling and dealings of the council. Give me a sword and stick me on the battlefield. "Tell Colin I have nothing to wear."

Cassidy gave me an overly bright smile. I wanted to pull her hair out. "Good thing you have me." She danced to my closet and returned with a black garment. "You should definitely wear this."

I took one look at the dress and thought about screaming for help. It would only take Zavier two seconds to bust through the adjoined door. I smiled as I envisioned Cassidy's face at seeing Zavier. It was temptation enough to follow through and ruffle Miss Perfect's feathers. She was the type of girl who cowered behind a man, always waiting for one to step in and save her.

Shaking the thoughts from my head, I stared at the dress. I'd never seen it before. This was obviously a plant, and by the way Cassidy was coveting the material, I was about to tell her she should wear it.

But in walked Colin. "I know that look. And no. You can't get out of this. I was planning to have you at my side this evening."

Cassidy slipped out of the room, leaving me alone with Colin. "Take Cassidy. She's dying to be at your side."

"Skylar," he warned.

I scowled. "I'm not a child. You don't have to scold me."

"Then stop throwing a tantrum and get dressed. Zavier will bring you down in an hour whether you're ready or not."

I choked back a laugh. "Is that a threat?"

"If it gets you downstairs on time, yes. No tricks or glamour."

"You take the fun out of everything." I decided not to tell him I wasn't speaking to the council.

"If I have to suffer through the next few hours, so do you," he said dryly.

I smiled, but it was strained. "Or we could both indulge in a rune."

"No magic." He turned toward the wall that connected my room to Zavier's. "Did you hear that, Zavier? No funny business, or I'm holding you personally responsible," Colin hollered.

"Loud and clear," Zavier's voice traveled from the other side of the wall.

"You're lucky we're related," I told Colin.

He grinned. "I'll let you curse my name as you get ready." He turned to leave, but paused at the door. "Oh, Liam is going to be there. Will that be a problem?"

"We'll find out. Why do we host these dumb parties anyway?" I hated them when I was little, and I despised them even more as an adult.

"It's tradition, Sky. Gives them hope, a semblance of normalcy that life can be as it once was."

"But it can't," I argued. "Why pretend otherwise? Life will never be like what it was before."

"Maybe so, but we can try." His fingers drummed on the doorframe before slipping out into the hall.

I sighed and stared at the dress lying on my bed. It seemed like wasted energy for someone to have crafted such an elegant dress. There were people in the village who needed clothes far more than I needed a dress. Heartsick, I knew there was little time for grieving and even less for comfort.

❧

FORTY-FIVE MINUTES LATER, I was draped in frilly silk, pacing my room. I nibbled on my lower lip, wrestling with this insane idea to climb over the terrace and scale down the three stories to ditch the party. It wasn't like it was the first time I'd done something reckless, but there usually isn't a house full of people. Or the six-foot plus warden next door with an unusual six-sense where I was concerned.

The evening air was balmy, making the room feel like a sauna. My skin was slightly pink and flushed, and there were beads of sweat dripping between my breasts. A knock sounded on the door, and I drew my eyes away from the balcony. "Come in," I called, swiping the moisture at the base of my neck.

The door squeaked open and Zavier dwarfed the archway. Tonight, he wasn't wearing his usual boring warden getup. A silver shirt stretched over his chest, nearly matching his eyes. He stilled the second he caught sight of me, his eyes running over the length of my body. When his final gaze connected with mine, the room got a whole lot hotter. "Wow. You look—"

Heart failure.

"Don't you dare say beautiful. That is too cliché."

His eyes were unwavering and intense, like the man. "Okay, how about exceptional?"

My lips curled. "It will do." I fidgeted in the dress, dying to get out of the silky material and into something less…actually, something more. I felt exposed. "I hate these things."

I stubbornly refused to watch Zavier approach.

But what was the point?

My body was already responding.

A cool wash of male filled the air, and made me think of things that were outlawed in the Bay.

"I never would have guessed."

I laughed, the sound of it raspy. "Liar."

The tread of his shoes hit the hardwood floors. Then he was standing beside me, golden skin glowing in the moonlight. His face was impossibly attractive. The warden was drop-dead gorgeous, but damn if I would ever admit that to his face.

My heart gave an odd, dangerous heave, before I gave up trying to fight this feeling inside me. Reaching up, I ran my hands over his chest. I wasn't sure what came over me, but I had to touch him, drawn to him like a love charm. "I'd much rather spend my time in here than downstairs at some stale party, talking about the security of the Bay." I moved into him, and kept moving until my body molded into his, my arms twining around his neck like ropes.

He arched a sexy brow.

Heat washed through me as I met the liquid silver gaze.

That was it. On impulse, I lifted on my toes and pressed my lips to his, brushing, retreating, brushing, before sinking warm against him.

A sound of seduction escaped my mouth, a shimmering promise of more to come. The party was forgotten. Everything was forgotten, everything but Zavier.

His scent, the subtle, yet unforgettable hint of fragrance that was all man and full of secrets, carried in with the warm breeze. It stirred something inside me, tangling my senses in a hot, satin punch of need.

I sighed, my fingers skimming into his hair as he started to ease away.

"You ready?" he murmured.

Zavier's dark voice wrapped around me, making my skin prickle with awareness. I grimaced. "Not a chance."

MEMBERS of the council and their families were gathered in the great room, vampires, witches, and humans all under one roof. These events made me uneasy, and tonight was no different. I was tense, waiting for the madness to descend. Soft music played from the corner of the room, a young man strumming on the keys of a makeshift piano. Instruments were scarce in the Bay, and the smooth melody of music put people in high spirits.

Appetizers and drinks were being offered and shuffled around. I grabbed two flutes of port off the tray. "Here, have a drink and loosen up," I said, putting a glass in Zavier's hand.

He scowled, and I expected a lecture about drinking on the job. "We got trouble coming."

Trouble already. This night might be looking up. "When

don't I?" I mumbled, pulling a long swig from the glass before turning around.

Damn.

Liam.

Not the kind of trouble I was hoping for.

He looked dashing, his sandy hair combed back, and the crisp white shirt stretched over his chest. "Can we talk?" The insinuation was that it was a personal matter.

"Now?" A party with every council member's eyes on me was probably the worst time to discuss what Liam wanted to talk about.

His eyes moved over my head, giving Zavier the stink eye. "In private," Liam added.

Zavier's hand was at the small of my back. "Not happening."

I positioned myself in the middle, in case one of them decided to take a cheap shot. "Liam, this isn't the time or place."

He exhaled. "I know that, and I had no intention of speaking to you, but then I saw you."

Shit.

I took another sip, wishing I had a buzz. It would make dealing with this situation less stressful. "Liam. I don't want things to be awkward between us."

"I know it has been weird, but maybe we both needed space. You look beautiful by the way."

Zavier snorted, remembering I had told him how cliché being called beautiful was.

I gave Zavier a jab in the gut with my elbow, but it was like hitting a brick wall. "Thanks, but a few sweet words aren't going to fix things between us, Liam. I meant what I said. I want us to be friends."

"Friends," Liam echoed. There was hurt and anger etched in his handsome features.

I stepped forward, closer to the warden who had always been a part of my life. "Would that be so bad?"

His emerald eyes searched my face. "There's no changing your mind, is there?"

Silence. I didn't know what else to say.

Liam reached out, taking my hand. "I thought you cared about me. Please, I can't lose you." He had lowered his voice.

Begging was not becoming on Liam, and Zavier didn't think so either. He stepped forward. "Don't make this harder."

Zavier's interference didn't sit well with Liam, hardness snapped into his expression like a switch. "Let me guess. You're the new flavor of the month. Don't worry, she'll get bored of you, too. It is what Skylar does." And then Liam stalked across the great room.

"Asshole," I muttered, downing the rest of my glass. I was beginning to understand that the damage was done, and Liam and I might never be the same again. I would have to live with it.

To his credit, Zavier didn't flinch, but his lips twisted. "You look like you can use this." He handed me his drink. "What did you ever see in that douchebag?"

That question was running through my head, too.

It was hard for me to get into the social mood. One of my good friends had been brutally murdered, and each day that went by with nothing done ate away at me. I wanted a few hours with my coven. Maybe even indulge in some evil ways to kill the bitch responsible.

And get drunk.

I was well on my way to the last as I picked up my third glass. The confrontation with Liam had left me unnerved and confused. What kind of person, was I? I had warned Liam that I didn't have it in me to fall in love. He hadn't believed me, had been determined to change my mind, but the truth was, Liam hadn't been the one. And that had hurt him.

A raven brow flicked upward as I put the glass to my lips, thinking to down my guilt, sadness, and anger into booze. "Am I going to have to carry you out of here?" Zavier whispered near my ear.

"Admit it, you'd like that." He tended to manhandle me.

The grin on his lips was enough confirmation.

Colin appeared at Zavier's side, laying a hand on his shoulder before the warden could respond, Zavier's eyes still glinting with humor. "You can't hide behind Zavier all night."

"Why must you torture me?"

"Because deep down, you have a caring heart and want the best for Frisco Bay, and that is what the mission of the council is, regardless how ignorant most of the members are. You won't turn a blind eye at the first sign of trouble," Colin said.

"Fine." I sighed, looping my arm through my brother's. "You can parade me around the room, and I promise to smile, but don't ask me to keep my opinions to myself." Because like he pointed out, I did care about the Bay. And who knew what kind of information one of these stuffy council members might have.

I made the rounds with Colin, kept the fake smile on my lips until they hurt, and laughed at one miserable joke after another. The minutes dragged, making the night seem as if it would never end. I couldn't wait to blow this party and move onto important things—like the coven.

I sipped on my glass of port, taking it a bit slower. I would need a clear head if I were going to ditch this function later. I might have preferred night to morning, but I let a big yawn. A decent night's sleep for once might be in order. At least that was going to be my excuse for leaving the party. What I was going to be doing—sneaking off to the coven—was no one else's business…except the warden.

Speaking of the devil. Where the hell was my shadow? He hadn't been more than ten feet from me all night, and now that I needed to conspire with him, he was nowhere to be seen.

A chill chased down my spine as my eyes scanned the room. It was strange, as if someone had put a cloaking spell on him. I swore the shimmer of magic trembled in the air, and whether I wanted to admit it or not, there was this strange connection I'd felt with Zavier since our first kiss, as if he was somehow a part of me. That feeling was always inside, except for now.

I noticed it more because it was missing.

"Zavier?"

CHAPTER 16

Wafts of cool, fresh air drifted over my flushed face. "Zavier?" I called again. *Where the hell is he?* Goodie fucking gumdrops. The one time I needed him to be glued to my side, he was nowhere in sight.

What gives?

It wasn't like Zavier to slack in his duties.

A rush of wind and suddenly, the air was filled with fluttering bats, swooping down from the night. I gasped and ducked as the flying black creatures filled the hall and into the great room, their squawks piercing my ears in a deafening sound. I spun, watching them swirl around the guests, their shrieks of surprise and fear joining in the chaos.

And then, for no reason I could see, the herd of bats scattered, flying out the door as swiftly as they had come. An eerie silence descended upon the room, and I knew the mayhem wasn't over. Yep, it was only the prelude of problems with a capital P.

Vampires.

My mouth opened to scream an alarm, but I was too late. A

pale hand wrapped around my mouth, cutting off my warning. "Well, hello," a voice hissed in my ear as a vampire grabbed me from behind. "Just who I was hoping to run into. Must be my lucky day."

Sure as shit was.

I had to act fast. Lifting my fingers, I managed to touch the rune on my other forearm. Tingles charged the air, like little jolts of electricity, and the stake I summoned from the training room materialized in my grasp.

His fangs had extended and ran along the side of my exposed neck. "You're not what I expected, witch."

I got that a lot, and would have told him if his grubby paw weren't still attached to my mouth. Cocking back my arm, I embedded the wooden stake into his chest. The pythons holding me fell away, and I spun, seeing the startled expression on the Bitten's face. I wasn't done with him yet.

"Didn't anyone tell you to pick on someone your own size?" I kicked out my foot, hitting the top of the stake with my heel and sending the stake deeper into his chest. "Still feeling lucky?" I asked, my tone going dry. A sudden burst of light and ash exploded in my face. "Thanks for ruining a perfectly good dress, asshole."

With my heart lodged in my throat, I forced myself to stay calm. My eyes bounced over the madness that had descended into the great room, desperately searching for Zavier and Colin. I had to get out of here, lead the vampires away before anyone else got hurt. They had come for me, and in the back of my mind, I'd known this day was coming, but I had prayed there would be more time to prepare.

My gaze quickly found Colin. He had moved into warden-mode, ordering his guards to take down the vampires who had invaded Silent Bend and broken the rules, attacking both humans and witches. Hell, they had even attacked some of their own.

Completely messed up, but Lilith didn't care who got in her way. They were meaningless.

Picking up my stake from the ground where it had fallen with the vampire's ash, I wiped off the end with the drapes hanging over a nearby window. The housekeepers would be pissed, but in the scheme of things, my mess was nothing compared to the blood, bodies, and dead vampire ash.

I'd never had a warden give me the slip before. This was a first. Colin would blow a gasket, but then a terrifying thought hit me. What if Zavier was missing because he'd been hurt…or worse?

I refused to believe he was dead. No way. The man was too stubborn to die. I wouldn't let him. It only took a few seconds to wind into a whirlwind of worry. "Where are you?" I muttered.

As if he heard me, Zavier rounded the corner, shooting into the room. He looked formidable with the stake clenched in his hand. Not that he needed it to be a badass. It was part of his genetic makeup.

A bone of dread settled in my belly like rocks. Zavier's eyes went straight to me, and I opened my mouth to call his name. Before he could reach me, the lights began to flicker, and in a rapid sequence, they blew out, one after another. Sparks showered, raining from overhead, right before the room was submerged in utter darkness. People screamed. Zavier roared my name, but my feet stayed rooted.

Flutters of what felt like cold shadows weaved in and around me, giving me the willies. Throwing out my hand, I summoned a ball of light and tossed it into the air, shedding rays of glowing amber over the room.

Zavier cursed.

Somehow during the blackout he'd been able to find me, but he wasn't the only one. We were surrounded by vampires. "I hate party crashers," I grumbled, my back pressed to his.

A chorus of angry hisses vibrated through the room. Zavier wound our fingers together and groaned. "We should probably take this party outside."

I shot him a weary look. "Uh, a little too late. Do you think they want to capture or kill me?"

"At the moment, it doesn't matter. Neither is an option."

"I couldn't agree more, but that doesn't mean we can't kill them, right?"

He squeezed my hand. "I like how your mind works, minx."

"Traitor," one of the vampires growled, revealing his fangs.

What did he mean, traitor?

"That's the best you got?" Zavier said, cracking his neck. His words were like ringing for dinner. The vampires all launched themselves at Zavier, the hunger for the kill shining in their pale blue eyes.

As Zavier went into ninja-stance, I wondered where the other wardens were. It wasn't like them to abandon one of their own. It was against the handbook. Most of the guests had taken off for the hills, eager to find safety. The council wasn't made of warriors, but prestigious old men, my brother the exception. He had taken my father's place after his death.

I wasn't sure what was going on, but this attack on Silent Bend had been well orchestrated—something only Lilith had the brains and patience for. She had wanted to get him segregated, and I doubted it was for a tropical vacation.

One thing was certain. I couldn't leave Zavier to fight the mob of vampires alone. My muscles tightened as I tried to remember all the combat lessons Colin had drilled into me. It didn't take long for me to figure it out once the first one reached me; instinct kicked in. I blocked out all the craziness in the room and focused solely on the vampire in front of me.

I kicked my leg out, catching him in the stomach before he could reach me. The key with vampires was to get the jump on them, because it only would take a split second to lose track of the bloodsuckers. Their speed made it impossible for human eyes to keep track of.

But not true for Zavier.

He didn't seem to have any trouble following their sporadic movements, and why was that?

Something to ponder for another day. I needed to get this vampire off me. Spinning around, I threw out my arm in one clean sweep, catching the Bitten in the heart with my stake.

The vampire went up in ash.

I looked up, my eyes going straight to Zavier as he was pulling out his stake from the last vampire. Impressive, but I should have expected no less. I could only see the side of his face, but that alone was enough. His eyes brightened, the veins surrounding them darkening like spilled ink. Two fangs grew, extending much like a vampire, gleaming in the spilled moonlight.

I sucked in air, a gasp that to human's ears wouldn't have been heard, but Zavier angled his head a fraction of an inch toward me. Pain streaked across his eyes as mine locked directly with his.

My head shook back and forth, refusing to believe what my eyes were seeing. He couldn't be—not a vampire—could he?

I should have known. How many times had my lips touched his? His essence had always been blind to me, hidden.

My suspicion of him being different was beginning to make sense, but this?

Traitor. That was what the vampire had called him. A traitor.

I took a step backward. "You're a vampire?"

His gaze dropped, the fangs receding and his eyes returning to normal. "Half," he corrected.

Oh. My. God.

My warden was a vampire.

He had deceived me—deceived us all.

"You son of a bitch." I could feel myself beginning to shake, and stinging tears gathered in my throat. Using all my strength, I channeled the hurt into rage. "You lied to me. You made me think you cared about me. You let me sleep with you."

"It's not what you think. I had to." His hand reached out to touch my cheek.

"Don't." I slapped his away. "Don't you ever put your hands on me again."

"Will you listen for a minute?" he growled.

"It all makes sense now, why I could never get a read on you. How could you lie to me? You made me trust you?" It didn't matter that he had fought and killed vampires to protect me. I was beyond being able to see anything but Zavier as a vampire.

"Minx—"

My hand cracked across his face before he could finish whatever he had been going to say. "Don't ever call me that again. In fact, I never want to see you again. Get the hell out of my house!"

"Skylar, let me—"

I shoved past him and fled. I didn't care if there were still vampires inside the compound. I didn't care that they could be camping out in my room. The only thing I cared about was getting as far away from Zavier as I could.

For once, he didn't follow me. It was the smartest thing he'd done since becoming my warden.

CHAPTER 17

I refused to speak to Zavier. Not since I barricaded myself in my room.

Hands shaking, I folded my arms and paced the length of the floor. I couldn't believe I had trusted him, let him into my life, into my bed. He had made a fool of me, and I was no one's fool.

Squeezing my eyes shut, I slammed my fist against the wall, not caring about hurting myself. I was already in pain. There were no limits to my anger. There was this tear inside me, and each breath I took, it ripped a bit more, a hole I wasn't sure could ever be filled.

I'd left the terrace window open and the wind whipped through my bedroom, flames in the hearth jumping in rage, licking the brick surrounding the fireplace as magic trembled in the air.

My chest spasmed as I thought of us in the throes of passion, him kissing my neck, touching my body, leaving me trembling.

I dropped down to the edge of the bed, letting my head fall

into my hands. Was he punishing me? Was it all an act to get close to me? And I had been putty in his hands. His secrets had been so much bigger and worse than I ever imagined.

My head hurt thinking about it. He had known how I'd felt about the Berkano vampires and vampires in general. He had known what they'd done to my mother. It didn't matter he was only half a bloodsucker, what mattered most was he had deceived me.

There were so many lies that the truth was covered in a tangle of webs. His explanations meant nothing. His reasonings were shot to shit, not that I had given him the opportunity to explain himself, but in my current state, I wasn't calm enough to listen.

Dazed, I stripped out of the dress, dropping it into the hearth. The fabric quickly caught fire, setting the room aglow as the ferocious flames hungrily ate the silky material.

I didn't sleep.

How could I when my mind and body were so torn up? I blew off the coven meeting, unable to move. My eyes open, I stared into the darkness, not really seeing anything. The only real thing was the pain in my chest that doubled with each heartbeat.

Angry tears burned at the back of my throat, a familiar feeling I'd avoided for years, since the death of my parents. It overtook me, and before I could stop them, tears were falling down my cheeks in messy streaks.

Oh, God. I was crying over Zavier, breaking a promise I'd made to myself, and I hated it. Hated that I cared more than I wanted to admit. I had allowed myself to fall in love. Bastard.

☙❧

A KNOCK SOUNDED on the door, and I groaned. Everything hurt —bones, tissues, and muscles. I rolled out of bed. "Who is it?" I asked, my voice dull and monotone. The last thing I wanted was company.

"Open up, Sky."

Colin. Of course he would send my brother. I stood on wobbly legs, and waved my hand in the air. The lock gave a click, and Colin walked in. "To what do I owe this pleasure?"

"Cut the sarcasm," he snapped. "What the hell is going on with you? Why have you shut yourself up in this room, and don't give me any lies. It's been two days since the attack."

A hysterical laugh escaped. "Oh, that's rich. Me. Lie. If you want the truth, talk to Zavier."

"I'm running on little sleep, I haven't eaten in two days, so I don't have time to play peacemaker between the two of you. Whatever asshat thing he has done, get over it. Or stop sleeping with every guard I assign you."

I recoiled as if he'd slapped me. My outrage was quickly replaced with heat. "Now who is the asshat?" I refused to cry. There was no way in hell I was going to shed a single tear over Zavier Cross.

Colin ran a hand over his scruffy face. "Shit. I'm sorry, Sky. I didn't mean to lash out at you. These last few days are starting to take a toll on me. Every time we've got a handle on the situation, we get smacked in the face with three more problems. It feels as if it is never going to end and only gets worse. I don't know what I'm doing anymore. I don't know how to keep us safe, and our control is slipping."

These were all things I didn't want to hear, but I couldn't hide from what was to come forever. Each day, each hour, each second I did hide away, things only escalated. The Berkano vampires were closing in, gathering what they needed and building their ranks. And here I was, sitting in my room, ranting over a broken heart. There were bigger obstacles that needed my attention. I had let Zavier distract me from my task, even if only for a few days. And now knowing he was part of the problem and could be working for the other side, I had a decision to make. And I needed to make it now.

"Zavier is a vampire," I blurted out, wringing my fingers.

Colin's head whipped up so fast his face blurred. "What did you just say?"

"The warden you assigned to me, the one who is your *friend*, he is a Bitten."

"Half," said a dark voice from the doorway. Zavier. "She found out," he said to Colin, leaning a shoulder against the frame.

I wanted to hurl a bolt of fire and incinerate Zavier on the spot. Then his words penetrated the haze of red that had suddenly taken over at the sight of him. My eyes slanted, volleying between Colin and Zavier. "You knew!" I flung at Colin.

My brother's lips thinned. "Considering how you feel about vampires, I thought it was best he not tell you."

"*You* decided. But you never thought to tell *me*," I snapped.

"It wasn't a decision I made lightly, but yes, it was for your safety," Colin explained, but I was having none of it.

The candles in the room began to flicker as the energy in the air thickened. "I'm so sick of hearing those words."

Colin's eyes darkened as they did when he held his power strong and steady. My brother was letting me know not to challenge him. "You needed a guard who could keep a better eye on you. Don't think I don't know about your late-night meetings with the other witches. You have a coven you never told me about," he hurled. We had both kept secrets.

I shot a glare at Zavier, accusation flaring in my eyes and little sparks of magic dancing over my skin. "You told him."

Zavier hadn't budged from his lazy position of leaning on the doorframe. "I didn't have to tell him anything. He already knew."

Argh. I was fuming—at them both.

"Zavier has the necessary skills to look out for you," Colin justified.

I hated being ganged up on. "Was it also part of your plan to have him seduce me?"

"He seduced you?" Colin's narrow gaze moved from my face to Zavier.

Finally, his anger was directed at the proper target, but I waved a hand in the air, dismissing the claim. Zavier hadn't done anything I hadn't wanted to do. "It doesn't matter. You lied to me. Both of you lied to me. I can't fathom what you were thinking assigning him as my warden. Why?"

Colin sighed, and I could see in his eyes that he only wanted what was best for me. "I thought keeping the truth from you was better than you knowing Zavier was part vampire. Your impression of them is jaded, regardless that not every vampire is a killer. Zavier wasn't even raised by vampires. He was outcasted, and has no loyalty to Lilith."

The mention of her name sent a hot haze of hatred through me, blurring my vision. What had been done was done. Even if Colin realized his mistake, there was no going back, and for now, I only wanted to be alone.

My hand flung out, and the door to my room catapulted open. The windows began to shake, and the floorboards under my feet trembled. I was quickly losing my hold on my temper. "Get. Out. Both of you."

"Skylar," Colin pleaded. When I didn't budge, he shook his

head. "Fine. Go ahead and sulk in your room." He swept out in hurried strides.

Zavier stepped further into my space, his brows furrowing as if he wanted to say something more.

The shock and hurt had worn off, and I'd moved straight into pissed off. He had about two seconds to walk out that door before I did something I might later regret. I wasn't thinking clearly, rage consuming my every thought.

"Regardless of what you're feeling, it won't stop me from doing my job. You're still under my protection." Shaking his head, Zavier turned and left.

On a moment derived of pure raw emotion, I flicked my wrist, the door slamming shut behind him, followed by the click of a lock.

"Funny. You know a lock won't keep me out," Zavier said from the other side of the door.

I lost it, letting out a scream of frustration. My white-hot desire for retribution increased tenfold, and nothing was going to stop me, certainly not Zavier Cross.

CHAPTER 18

Flames crackled in the grate as I lay on the bed. The next few days blurred together. I rarely slept. And it was catching up to me, but I was avoiding more than the half-vampire in the next room.

I wasn't strong enough to deal with Lilith's invasion into my subconscious, not when I was so turned up inside, but I could only put off the inevitable for so long.

Exhaustion got the best of me. I closed my eyes, dreaming of a cave with gold floors and sparkling jewels scattered in the stone. The one place I wanted to evade.

Lilith sat on an obsidian throne, staring at all those jewels, her dark beauty unearthly and fearsome.

Beyond the walls, screams echoed in pain and torture, crying out for help. Fear feathered down my spine. There were other sounds. Moans of pleasure. The air was hot with the stench of metal, lust, and death.

And the cave walls ran with blood.

It was the sensation of strong arms pulling me into a warm embrace that woke me from the confusing nightmare. Trembles racked my body as I struggled to banish the sounds and images from my head.

"Shh, Sky," Zavier murmured, a soft hand stroking down my hair. "She can't touch you now."

"What are you doing in here?" I choked out. I hadn't forgotten I was still furious at him, regardless how amazing it felt to be held in his arms. The shakes began to reside, and my hand clutched at him as I struggled to regain control of myself.

He shifted on the bed, brushing aside the sweat-drenched sheet, and my arms tugged him back down. I didn't want him, but I didn't want him to leave.

What a quandary I was in. When he settled beside me, I sighed, resting my head on his bare chest. I couldn't deny he enticed a feeling of being protected I needed. Tomorrow, I might be kicking myself for the moment of weakness, but for tonight, I was going to find peace. I'd seen too much death. "She won't stop looking for me," I whispered.

"No, she won't," he murmured. "But you're safe."

"Am I?" I concluded that maybe I trusted the warden more than I hated his guts. I'd been unable to stop the magnetic pull to him. I didn't understand it—the connection I felt to him. My brain wanted to despise the vampire, but my heart wanted to tangle itself more and more with the man.

I knew I couldn't have one without the other.

He pressed a kiss on the top of my head. "I swear to you, Skylar, I would never do anything to hurt you."

It was lunacy…but I believed him, even when I didn't want to. I was being hunted by a power-hungry vampire, yet the only time I felt safe was when I was with Zavier. It irritated me, knowing I relied on him. I didn't need anyone, let alone a half-vampire.

And yet, my body ached to be close to his.

I had to put a stop to this. "I'm okay," I said, pulling out of his arms, regardless how empty I was without them. "You don't need to stay and babysit me."

Those dark brows shot up. "Is that what you think I'm doing?"

A flare of anger speared through me, and I concentrated on that emotion, refusing the others from surfacing—the softer more dangerous feelings. "Just because we slept together once doesn't mean I care about you. It was nothing—a meaningless one-night stand." Lie after lie spewed from my lips. If I said it with enough conviction and anger, maybe I could make it true.

"Bullshit. Do you want me to prove what a liar you are?" he rasped. Without warning, I found myself flat on my back, with Zavier pressed on top of me.

My bones melted at the feel of his delicious body pinning me to the mattress, but I jutted my chin out in defiance. "It takes a liar to know one. You think I would let you touch me now that I know what you are?"

Hurt and anger flashed in his eyes, but turned quickly hard and cold as the deep sea, again hiding the truth from me. "I wouldn't have pegged you for shallow."

Now it was my turn to be hurt, but he was right. I wasn't that kind of person...normally. It was just he was associated with the very beings I grew up loathing—the one who hunted me. Yet to be fair, he couldn't control his birthright any more than I could control mine. It was biased of me to judge him for it, but the bastard had lied to me, deceived me, used me. My feelings no longer mattered. "We had sex. End of story."

Angling his head to the side, he extended the fangs he had kept hidden from me. He leaned toward me, and the flash of fangs touched on my skin, drifting over the pulse hammering at the base of my throat, but I refused to yield. My hands curled into fists at my side, and I squeezed my eyes closed.

Shit.

Bad idea.

With my eyes shut, I relied on my other senses, all jumping to life under Zavier's hypnotic caress. The sound of his quick breathing. The fresh waterfall scent that clung to his skin, permeating the air around him. The seductive thrill left behind on my neck as his fangs and tongue took turns teasing the beating vein.

"I've longed to taste the rich nectar of your blood. I shouldn't crave it, but it doesn't change the fact that whenever I'm near you, the temptation is there," he whispered, his warm breath tickling the sensitive spot behind my ear.

He had a power over my body—an influence I couldn't control or prevent. "Zavier." I shivered, in an almost plea that could have been a yes or a no. I lifted my fingers to press against his chest with every intention to push him away, but then my lashes fluttered open and I realized too late what a mistake that had been.

His silver eyes burned bright, fingers tightening at my hips, and the thread of his control was on the edge of unraveling. "You belong to me."

Did I?

Could I?

There was no denying I wanted him to kiss me, to touch me, to make me feel alive instead of this dead coldness inside me. I wanted him to take away the anger, the pain, the hurt. Only he could do it. It made no sense, but little did.

I hated him.

But I wanted him.

I detested the vampire.

But loved the man.

My fingers curled into his shirt, neither pushing him away nor pulling him closer. I lay there, poised on the edge of a cliff. Did I jump or scamper away from the ledge?

"This is for your protection, minx," he rasped.

My lips twitched. "You seducing me is for my own protection? That's a new one."

"I don't know whether to bite you or spank you."

"Surprise me." Had that come out of my mouth? What the hell was wrong with me? I needed to have my brain scanned for defects.

His tongue ran over the vein, leaving a wet path down my neck. "Mine."

The possessiveness in his voice made me quiver.

With a harsh groan, he plunged his fangs into my skin, and my head fell back, sinking deeper into the feather pillow. My legs wound around his waist, and I arched up, pressing my hips into his.

Gods.

Something happened.

The stars aligned. The earth shifted. I lost my mind.

Power slammed into me, swimming in my veins as Zavier took the sweet warmth of my blood into his mouth. This was wrong, against so many rules, but in the height of pure ecstasy, I didn't care. I only knew I didn't want him to stop.

My arms wound around him, holding tight as tiny jolts of electricity threw me over the edge as my body shattered into a million pieces. The orgasm was unexpected. He had barely touched me. Only a bite.

If I was given a second to think about what had occurred, I would be filled with shame, but Zavier had moved from sucking my neck to kissing me brainless. Where he was concerned, I had no control over my body or my feelings.

This was madness.

He captured my lips in a kiss, my skin flushing with the stain of arousal as heat curled within my body.

I didn't want romance or sweet nothings. What I wanted was hot, fast sex, no tangles of emotions, just speed and sweat. At least that was what I told myself. As always, Zavier knew what I wanted and needed before I did.

Nails raked over flesh as I used my teeth on his earlobe. I was rewarded as his body instantly responded, seeing the lightning streak of heat cloud his eyes.

But he didn't give me the hot and fast I sought. He caught me off guard, crushing his lips to mine in a slow, drugging kiss that left my limbs weak. With light fingers, he lifted the shirt over my head in a teasing exploration, my undergarments following.

I trembled with pleasure, blood racing. There was also a new desire I'd never experienced before. The hunger to feel his fangs buried deep in my flesh. I wanted it again, and the dark glory of it gushed through me, surging until passion drowned the anger and doubts.

"There might be darkness running through my blood, but it is you, minx, who has stolen my heart," he murmured in a raspy voice.

My gaze locked with his as he slid into me with one smooth stroke.

God almighty.

I would have sworn I was well rounded when it came to sex, but Zavier made me think there was so much more I had to learn. He touched me in dangerous places, pieces of myself I had deliberately shut off. Words whispered from my lips. I didn't know what I was saying, only that I couldn't stop them from tumbling out of me.

It was magic. There was no other way to describe what was shimmering through my body.

His pace was slow, drawing out the pleasure with the promise of paradise. I quickened my hips as they rolled upward to meet his, reaching for the bliss of release.

His fangs quivered over the vein in my neck, and I ached for him to take another bite, pressing my throat closer to his fangs just as my body erupted in shattering pleasure.

A red haze of lust tore through me as he yanked my mouth back to his, diving inside me, shooting me over the edge.

I exploded. Again.

CHAPTER 19

A misty glow fell over the room. We were entangled in the middle of the bed, Zavier running gentle fingers over the white rune scrolled onto the flesh of my forearm.

My lips glided over his jaw, down the column of his throat to the beating pulse. I froze, my hand going to my own neck. Zavier had bit me, he had taken my blood, and in the process, we had broken one of the sacred laws of the treaty.

What had I done? I'd had sex with a vampire. The best sex of my life. But it had been more, and that was the problem. There were no excuses for my actions, no sane explanation, and that was it. Zavier made me feel unstable, as if I would lose my footing, but in the same breath, he would keep me from falling.

It made no sense.

So I needed to make sense out of it.

My eyes went to his fingers and to the white marks he was tracing on my arm. I blinked. There was a new rune, one I hadn't drawn, and that was the mark he was outlining. "What did you do to me? My heart and head are at odds. My entire body is feeling off. I can't explain it. And this..." I lifted my hand in the air and turned it from side to side, examining the new mark. "How did this get there?"

"You don't like it?" he asked, shifting on the bed and looping an arm behind his head.

"I'm unsure. It depends on what it is, what it does."

"It's the mark of a mate—a symbol that you belong to another."

"You marked me?"

"I didn't do it alone." He held up the inside of his arm, exposing an identical mark. "I am as much yours as you are mine. You're my mate, Skylar."

I lifted my head, resting my chin on his chest. "Excuse me? Did you say mate?"

"How much of vampires do you know? Not the vampires of now, but before the Rift?"

My expression hardened. "I don't see why that matters. Can you back up a step?"

He tucked a strand of loose hair behind my ear, affection in his eyes. "I'm trying. You want answers. I'm giving them to you. What happened between us wasn't just a hot tumble in the sheets. For centuries, vampires have been known to have mates—human, witch, or vampire, there are no limitations between races. I knew you were meant to be mine from the moment I saw you during my training."

My brain thought back. I had no recollection of him. "I was a teenager then."

"You were. And I waited."

I made a sound of impatience. "This is strange for me. I still don't know if I can trust you, yet I have these feelings for you I can't make sense of. And the only person I can blame is you."

A small smile lifted at the corner of his lips. "I wasn't ready for you either, if that makes you feel any better. Your emotions and feelings are so strong. Everything you do is with so much passion. It took me by surprise. Still takes me by surprise."

"What is this between us? Why do I feel so different when I'm with you? It is more than because of who you are or this mark, but I'm not certain. How did this happen?" *Without me even realizing*, I added in my head.

"Your blood has a different meaning and effect on me—a potent one. Had your veins not filled with the essence of who you are—a witch—the bond would have only been one sided, but the second my fangs connected with your magical blood, the ancient tides awakened within us. There is no spell or curse that can sever the link we've created."

I was pretty sure I stopped breathing.

He was talking about forever.

I was mated to a half-vampire.

Fuck balls. What have I done?

He had lied to me. Abused my trust. And yet…

I found I still loved him. I was in love with Zavier.

The answer brought an end to my internal dialogue, and my breathing became labored, panic clamping down on my chest. It was the reason his betrayal hurt so much, more than Colin's. How had I let this happen? It couldn't. I wasn't ready to be in love with someone, much less mated.

His hands came to frame the sides of my face. "Skylar. It is going to be okay."

"You can feel that, can't you? What is going on inside me?" I asked softly.

He nodded. "I can." Picking up my hand, he placed it over his heart. "And if you give yourself a moment, you'll realize you can also sense mine."

"What if I don't want to?" I gritted. "I have enough going on inside me without tangling up with your emotions, too."

He flashed a smile filled with dangerous intent. "It doesn't work that way. You can learn to control it, weed through what's mine and what's yours, but the bond has already been solidified."

Just like that.

One wild, incredible night, and our paths were intertwined —our future cemented.

It might have been our fates all along, neither of us with the power to stop it. Not that it mattered now. "So that's it? There's nothing we can do?"

He arched a brow. "Are you trying to get rid of me already?"

I shrugged. "Just want to know my options."

"You have an eternity to explore them all."

"An eternity, huh?" I turned on my side, laying my head on my hands and staring at him. "What the hell have I gotten myself into? This is all happening too fast."

His eyes shimmered in the dark room as he followed my movements. "It isn't exactly how I planned this to happen. Fate often takes things out of our control."

My forehead wrinkled as I frowned. "I don't believe in fate. I believe we make our own destiny."

"Then it was your destiny to be mine." He took the pad of his thumb and rubbed it over my bottom lip, causing it to tingle. "I know this isn't what you dreamed about or even wanted, but know I wouldn't take it back for a second. You're mine, and I'm not letting you go."

I tried not to be affected by the sheer possessiveness in his tone, but it was impossible. My heart cartwheeled, and since I was still processing the new status of my life, I turned the conversation to a less emotional topic. "Did my brother know we were mates?"

"I'd rather not talk about your brother while we're in bed, but no, he doesn't know."

More secrets. How many more would I uncover?"

He shook his head. "It isn't like that. I don't want there to be anything between us—no liesno mysteries. I want to protect you, but I also understand your need for justice. I won't stand in your way."

"Are you sure you can't read my mind?"

His lips twitched. "There are many times I wish I could."

"I can't decide if I still hate you."

"You don't," he said with grinning arrogance. "You never hated me, but I am sorry I caused you grief."

It was hard not to believe him when I could sense a piece of him inside me. The barrier that had prevented me from being aware of his essence was gone, and a part of me was afraid of what I would see, but I'd never been a coward. I wasn't going to start today.

I let the flood of his emotions invade inside me, and I gasped. There was light and darkness within him, and I could feel the struggle between the two, but what stood out the most was the unwavering love he felt for me. It robbed me of air. I'd never known someone could feel that way about me, wasn't sure I had wanted anyone to. But now that my soul had been wrapped in it, I never wanted the warmth to end.

His hand moved to my chest, directly over my thumping heart. "I want to hear you say what I feel in your heart."

I hesitated. "What makes you think I love you?" He was asking for more than just words; he wanted forgiveness, acceptance. Could I give him everything he wanted?

His smile traveled up to his eyes. "You might not be ready to admit it, but I can wait. Because I love you."

"You love me?" I whispered, even though I knew the answer.

He nodded. "I do. With all my heart."

His confession was going to make what I had to harder.

⚉

THE NIGHT WAS TAINTED with the promise of death, and the moon was clouded by fog. My cloak dragged on the ground as I fled from Silent Bend and into the woods. I ran with my heart soaring and the brisk wind slapping my flushed cheeks. A tickle of mist dampened the forest floor.

I had waited until Zavier was fast asleep, before I had slipped on my boots and cloak. The coven was waiting for me, and I couldn't abandon them again, not when we needed each other more than ever. This battle with Lilith was going to end. Tonight, we acted.

He trusted me to stay in his arms, but no matter how I felt about the half-vampire warden, I had a promise to keep above all else. Zavier had understood that, just as I hoped he would understand when he awoke alone.

There was no denying my heart was heavy, but I pushed aside the clog of emotion and jutted out my chin. I concentrated on the solitude of the woods and what I had planned for Lilith. The run made me feel lighter and clearer in the mind, my purpose and destiny set out in front of me, a path illuminated by will and determination.

I was feeling more like myself as I moved soundlessly through the woods, invincible and reckless. The sense of freedom I hadn't felt in years returned. Sadly, it was short-lived.

Something hissed low and deadly behind me.

I wasn't alone.

And this time, I was damn sure it wasn't Zavier lurking in the woods, nor would he suddenly appear to save me.

"Shit," I mumbled, stealing a glimpse over my shoulder. It was impossible to tell which direction it had come from. Vampires and full moons went together like potatoes and corn.

This was not how I'd imagined my night would go, but it was becoming abundantly clear I had to pull out some superior butt-whooping skills. What a kick in the gut, knowing I was out here alone, without backup. Go figure. The one time Zavier didn't stalk me.

I quivered with power, knowing I'd never make it to the cottage tonight—never warn my sisters—never get the chance to weave a spell to end the vampire queen. If anything, I needed to keep my attacker's focus on me. The little cottage might be cloaked in magic, but Lilith had already proven to be clever and deceitful. I had to lead the vampires as far from the coven as possible. I would protect Jenna, Bailey, and Raine with my life.

I spread out my arms in invitation. "What are you waiting for? You want me, come and get me."

"Thought you'd never ask." Out of the darkness, a shadowy blur streaked around the trees, moving too fast for me to track. One second, I was standing under a canopy of leaves. The next, I was hauled backward, pinned against the trunk of a tree. A flare of annoyance lit up inside me before waning into stark terror as I stared into the vibrant eyes of Aeron.

Holy mother of God.

For a moment, I couldn't move; my brain went kaput. Aeron was Lilith's son, and one of the most feared vampires in the Bay. Just my luck.

"That was too easy," Aeron sneered, his tongue flashing over his fangs.

"You keep forgetting the rules," I reminded him.

He tilted his head to the side, eyes glued to the pulsing vein at my neck. "Times change."

The bark from the tree dug through the material of my cloak, rubbing against my skin. Fear finally gave way to instinct. I remembered I wasn't a helpless female; I was a witch. The power I let loose seared along my skin and swam in my blood, singing like raw nerves up my body.

It happened so fast. Good thing vampires liked speed.

The knife tucked into my boot flew to my hand and I struck, narrowly missing Aeron's eye. It wouldn't kill him, but it would leave one hell of a reminder. The vampire gave a furious cry of pain, and he released me just as I wanted...sort of.

With the blade still embedded in his cheek, Aeron tossed me like a Frisbee. I hit the cold ground with jarring impact, pain radiating through my spine. I lifted my head, knowing the vampire would recover a hell of a lot faster than me. Shoving off the forest floor with my palms, I sat up.

"That wasn't very nice, little witch," Aeron spat, dropping the blade in the grass beside me.

I shoved a handful of hair out of my face. "Where did you get the impression I was nice?"

He laughed, and the sound sparked a flame of rage.

Blood dripped down my arm as I got to my feet, stumbling slightly. "You think that's funny? I'll give you something to laugh about." The bravado in my voice was an act, because inside I was quaking.

There was only two ways this night was going to end, and I was deathly afraid I knew what my fate would be.

Aeron wasn't alone. Through the dark trees, brilliant blue eyes popped out in a chain reaction. I was surrounded, and dread seized me.

Now what, Sky?

Maybe this was a blessing in disguise. Maybe this was my chance to kill the vampire queen face to face. But I couldn't fight them all and live. The Berkano vampires might have gotten what they wanted, but I vowed to stake Lilith the first chance I got, and I wasn't going to walk into their den voluntarily.

There was a streak of movement to my right, followed by a slapping of metal like a bullet over the silent night. My brain was slow to process what had occurred, and then I glanced down. There was a pair of shackles cuffed around my ankles.

What the—?

I lifted one foot, testing the durability. *Shit.* It was one thing to be captured by the bloodsuckers, and another thing to be their prisoner. I tried to summon a bolt of magic. To my unpleasant surprise, nothing happened.

Not a drop of magic shimmered in my blood.

Assholes. How dare they neutralize my power?

Aeron laughed. "Those aren't budging, sweetcakes. They have a magic of their own."

With my powers diffused, I was defenseless and at the mercy of the Berkano vampires.

Shit.

Gauging the threat level and how much crap I'd managed

to get myself into, I stepped forward. "I won't go without a fight."

A chorus of hisses rang out around me, but it was Aeron who answered. "Now what fun would it be if you didn't? I'd be disappointed."

The burn of adrenaline moved from my chest, rippling into my veins. Cocking my arm back, I threw a punch, shocking us both by connecting with his jaw. Pain spread across my knuckles. Damn, I missed my magic.

"Bitch." His long fingers wrapped around my throat, nails digging into the skin, drawing blood. "Hitting isn't nice."

"Oh, and strangling me to death is?"

Aeron started to lift me off my feet. "You know you can't beat me in a fight."

My air supply was cut off. With a fierce effort, I strained against the power of the vampire and managed to wrench free. I tumbled to the ground and went down to my knees as my legs buckled, fingers digging into the grass. This was bad. Ultra-bad.

The vampire let out one long note of triumph.

I squeezed my eyes, waiting for the next blast and the next. Blood trickled over my face, but the blow never came. Instead, I was hauled roughly to my feet. Then I was flying through the woods, toward the caves in blinding speeds.

My flesh was battered, but as we entered the cave, a different kind of pain entered my body, the kind that left a scar on the soul. Desperation. Hopelessness. Terror. An intense maelstrom of emotions assaulted me. The caves were filled with lost souls, fraught for freedom.

The vampire holding me tossed me into a room, and I landed in a heap on the ground. Sudden and shocking pain, like a venomous and violent gash, flared within me. Even as I cried out, I saw the chambers—one after another, all witches. It was a flash, and when the vision was gone, so was the pain, but the ache inside me remained.

There was a terrible scream echoing off the rocky walls, like a thousand voices raised in fury.

Not a thousand.

Just one.

Mine.

CHAPTER 20

I woke to darkness instead of the thin morning sunlight, my cheeks damp and sticky, skin chilled. Inside, I was empty. I'd felt pain before, but the grief was so real, so fresh, like an open wound that couldn't heal.

Rolling over, I curled into a ball and prayed for the pain in my chest to pass as the first thought that filtered into my mind was Zavier. Was he racked with guilt? Going ballistic, wondering where I was? Or cursing me for breaking my promise?

My breath caught as a deep, unforgiving pang hit me in the heart. Ironic. Just as I found love, Lilith ripped it all away. The bitch would pay. If she was going to imprison me in her lair, I was going to make sure she never saw the light of day, or I would die trying.

Scrubbing my palms over my eyes, I blinked, slowly letting out the breath I'd been holding. My eyes roamed over the room.

It wasn't Caesars Palace.

No wonder my whole body ached. I was lying on a metal

slab, my ankles shackled to the cement floor, and my view was atrocious. Instead of the ocean and green hill of Silent Bend, I was staring at a row of vertical metal bars and the wall of a cavern.

A new sense of fear tangled inside me as the memories of last night tumbled to the surface, and my lip trembled, but I refused to shed a single tear. Not here in Lilith's domain. I would not show her an ounce of weakness, or a drop of fright.

Some of the details were hazy, before it had all gone black and I'd woken up in this cage where it hurt to breathe. The hardest part was knowing Colin and Zavier would be tearing up the Bay searching for me, not knowing where I was or what happened to me. My overprotective brother must be going batshit crazy with worry. The prospect of never seeing their faces again caused a fissure in my heart.

And now I had to face my fate, a prisoner of the vampire queen. What a hot mess.

I couldn't stay here. It was not part of the plan. This wasn't how I was supposed to defeat the vampire queen. It was supposed to be on *my* terms—*my* way—with *me* in control.

Despite the raw skin around my ankles from fighting, I sat up, forcing myself to move. The bands capturing my feet had stripped me from the one thing I'd always counted on, the one thing that had been given to me from my mom.

My magic.

Lilith had taken it from me.

Rage erupted, burning the air in my lungs like icy acid. It was no doubt a waste of my energy, but I had to attempt to use my power. Not trying would be stupid.

I concentrated, attempting to summon my magic, but the damn shackles around my ankles delivered one hell of a hair-singeing shock. I shrieked, glaring at the metal around my feet.

They didn't just prevent my abilities, but also delivered a kind of torture. Glutton for punishment that I was, I didn't give up. I tried again and again until I was blue in the face. It was hopeless. Until I got the cuffs off my ankles, my magic was useless, and that fueled my anger.

The next thing I knew, I was attacking the bars like a madwoman, doing more damage to my already-tender hands. "Son of a bitch," I moaned, shaking the sting from my fingers.

My chest squeezed painfully. Defeated and spent, I sat on the bed, dropping my head into my hands. Time went by in a haze. An hour or a day, I had no way of knowing, but nothing would stop me from trying to get the hell out of Lilith's vampire nest.

I sat straight up.

I'd been so consumed with my emotions I had forgotten what kind of opportunity being in Lilith's den provided me. This might not be the worst thing to happen, but it was pretty close. I'd been plotting and investigating a way into Lilith's lair. Now here I was, able to use this to my advantage and fulfill a promise that would also keep the Bay safe. A double win as far as I was concerned…if I succeeded. My odds were slim to none.

But there was no other choice.

I refused to be a puppet in Lilith's master plan of power and corruption. The big kink in my plan was I couldn't use magic. With my abilities neutralized, I had no way of getting out of here. No way to get to her. My fighting skills weren't accomplished enough to take out the vampire queen with my bare hands. I was good, but not godly.

The sound of footsteps neared before the face appeared. I conjured a million possibilities, but not one of them had been seeing Zavier. Imagine my surprise. Dark strands of hair fell over his forehead as his piercing eyes roamed over me from head to toe, eyes darkening when he saw the bruises on my face.

Seeing him, the beginnings of a hope materialized in the form of my six-foot-two half-vampire mate. I jumped to my feet and ran to the metal bars. "You found me. How did you find me?" I winced. The bitter burn at my ankles was a reminder of what I needed to do. I wasn't leaving without Lilith's dead heart in my hands.

"How are you feeling?" he asked in a level voice I barely recognized. His face was emotionless.

I waited for the sweep of emotions to hit me—happiness, relief, love—but there was only emptiness. I was confused. "I've been better," I said dryly. "Are you alone?" I expected there to be a storm of troops, chaos, but there was no noise, and only a very grim-looking Zavier. An uneasy feeling wormed into my belly.

"Yes," he replied curtly.

I studied him, wondering what was wrong, and the realization slowly began to sink in. This wasn't a rescue party. "I don't understand. How are you here? Am I dreaming?"

He placed both hands on the bars, parallel to his face. "No. This isn't a dream."

"You're not here to rescue me, are you?" I took a step back, away from this stranger who stood in front of me. Where was the man who had only hours ago held me gently in his arms, had made love to me, had made me his eternal mate? Told me he loved me.

This man had no warmth, was chilled to his core, hard and merciless like a vampire. He was everything I hated.

He gave a quick glance upward from the corner of his eyes

before a calculated gleam seeped in. "Depends on your definition of rescue, minx."

My mind couldn't believe what I was seeing, what I was hearing. This had to be a trick. Zavier had sworn to protect me. He would never do anything that would hurt me or put me in harm's way. I might have doubted who he was, but I never doubted his ability to keep me safe. So what was going on? "Zavier, help me," I pleaded.

He closed his eyes for a moment, knuckles tightening on the bars as if to get himself under control. "Lilith has summoned you. They will be watching us. Starting now. You're in her domain, and I can't always be there to save you, not without raising suspicion. My return already has a few brows arched," he murmured in a low voice.

Everything in my body froze, a thousand thoughts bombarding my mind. "I'm going to kill her, you know. If I don't stop her, the Bay will fall, and she will have won. I can't let that happen."

His hand flashed through the bars, gripping my wrist. "And if it kills you? What then? What about those who love you and who you will leave behind?"

Like him?

Finally, some damn emotion. "It will be meaningless if the Bay is ruined. Without a future, what is the point of love? I'm not even sure what's real anymore. Hours ago, you were telling me you loved me, and now, you're in the vampire's nest, helping them?"

Zavier's brows snapped together. "Let's get one thing clear. The only person I care about is you. I'm here because of you. I told myself I would never step foot in *her* domain again, yet here I am. I would go to the ends of hell to protect you."

"Then free me."

"I want nothing more than to take you out of here, but we wouldn't make it five feet without being attacked. I'm trying to keep us alive, and to do that, we have to play by her rules."

"I want to trust you, and my heart tells me you're a good man, but the fact you're allowed in the vampire's home makes me wonder if I know you at all."

He produced a key of sorts, and stuck it into the lock. "It doesn't matter. Lilith is waiting."

⚜

LILITH.

She wore a dress of fine silk, in a deep shade of red, jewels sparkling at her neck and fingers. While the rest of the Bay was wearing common clothes, the vampire queen draped herself in elegant fabrics and expensive stones.

She looked like a flame burning in the shadows. Seeing her, I wanted to rip the fangs from her mouth and cut off her pretty little head. Even then, it wouldn't be enough, wouldn't bring back the lives lost by her hand.

Eyes as dark as a summer's night met mine. "I'm so glad you finally joined me."

The shackles at my feet made something as easy as walking a challenge, and the rattling echoed with each step. "Like I had a choice."

"Yes, sometimes we all need a little push."

"You're delusional. There is nothing you can do or say to me that would ever make me help you," I spat, letting the words ring with my anger.

"I had sincerely hoped you would have changed your mind after seeing dear, sweet Abbey give her life for yours."

My brain clicked off. Something primitive and violent took

176

over. The hot blaze of magic filled my veins, but that was as far as it got, building like a geyser under the surface, ready to explode. If I had use of my powers, I would have obliterated her in this moment, not a care for my life or the vampires in the room. "You bitch," I seethed. Unable to stop myself, I lifted my palm into the air and swung, but before I could slap the queen across the face, she had moved to the other side of me.

"I wouldn't do that if I were you." She tsked.

"Go screw yourself. I won't help you reverse the Rift, and I sure as hell won't bear a vampire child."

"There is still time yet to change your mind. I'm in no hurry, and I'm feeling quite optimistic seeing as you've mated with one of my vampires." Her eyes shifted to Zavier at my side. In her voice, there was something exotic, a rhythm of speech that hinted at black sand beaches and blooming vines of poisonous flowers.

Enchanting.

I recognized the dust of magic. Lilith had a witch weaving spells of persuasion and obedience. Took a witch to know one.

Zavier said nothing, only stayed rigid, and I about lost my shit. "It doesn't matter what he is to me. I won't let him touch me, just as I won't allow your kind to kill anyone else. Enough blood has been shed."

Lilith glanced over her shoulder with a gleam in her bold iridescent eyes as she circled around me. "I'm a creature of the night. It's how we're meant to live, the natural order of vampires. I only intend to put things back the way they should be. Did you know I have more than one son? You'd make a truly beautiful daughter-in-law. Imagine the power your child would have with my blood and your magic."

I would rather not imagine such a thing. She was certifiably insane. How could Zavier stand there while she offered to let one of her bloodsucking sons knock me up? "It doesn't matter what room you give me in this fortress you've built underground. Nothing could make me agree to sire a vampire of your blood."

"You so sure about that? The funny thing about blood bonds is we often can't control our desires. I'm thinking a cell isn't the place for you here." Her fingers gripped me by the chin, holding my face steady. "I've heard of your gift, the ability to read a person's essence. It intrigues me, as do many powers bestowed upon witches."

Before I knew what her intent was, she leaned forward, pressing her lips to mine. Bile rose in my throat, but then, my mind became misty and muddled. Through the wisp of magic, I got a taste of her essence. Apparently, not all of my powers had been neutralized.

Air punched out of my lungs and I gasped, jerking back. "You're his mother," I hissed through my teeth. Lilith was Zavier's fucking mother. I refused to look at Zavier, for if I did, I knew I would attempt to kill the man who had betrayed me —lied to me. Again.

"Your warden's? Yes, Zavier is my son." Her cherry lips curved. "It's been quite convenient having someone on the inside."

"I just bet," I snarled. I didn't want to believe Zavier could have deceived me in the worse way possible. I had not only mated a vampire, but the son of the bitch who had killed my mother. Pain like I'd never felt since her death sliced through me in jagged slashes, ripping and tearing my insides apart.

I gasped, my lungs struggling for air. The room started to spin in dizzying circles as I sensed myself losing control of reality.

"Skylar," Zavier murmured, his cool hand sliding under my elbow.

I refused to look at him. How could I? A swarm of regret hit me in a tidal wave, strong enough to almost bring me to my knees. Lifting my chin, I focused on the dazzling eyes of Lilith.

She loved the chaos she caused between Zavier and me. "It is my understanding you've grown close to my son." Her sneer grew, that of a malevolent seductress. "Could it be you already carry his child?"

"Go to hell. I would die before I lift a finger to help you." And then, I spit in her face.

I expected instant death, but the vampire queen only wiped my slimy DNA off, managing to look regal while doing so. "It might not be wise to defy me. I will be queen of all, both day and night. Any who defy me would perish, starting with your brother."

Okay. No one threatened Colin and got away with it. I lunged, but two arms wrapped around my waist before I could even reach her.

Without waiting for an answer, she spun, leaving a trail of her scent behind as she walked down the hall, heels echoing over the stone.

Oh, I am going to kill her all right.

It was a mistake letting me live, one she would soon regret.

CHAPTER 21

I was shaking from head to toe in barely restrained rage. My head was swirling with every moment I'd ever spent with Zavier, wondering what part of it was real and what was part of a conspiracy against Division Fourteen. How could he have possibly fooled me? Did he even care about me at all? I had felt it—it had been so real. He had once told me he had abilities of his own. Did that include manipulating emotions? He had already proved he was able to know what I was feeling.

I wanted to cause him physical pain. His arms were still bound around me, keeping me from punching him, but as soon as he let me go…

"I know what is going through your head right now, and I am telling you to stop. You're letting her get to you, which is exactly what she wants," Zavier hissed into my ear. He grabbed my elbow, and spun me around to face him.

"You bastard." I hurled myself at him, my fist catching the right side of his jaw. My follow-up hit was deflected, and I found myself pinned against him, wrists clasped in his firm grasp.

"Dammit, Skylar," he growled. "If you would listen for a damn second."

My eyes move directly to his.

"Fine," he exhaled. "Have it your way." Like the barbarian he was, Zavier hauled me over his shoulder and carried me down a network of tunnels.

Tight-lipped, I kept my eyes fixated on the ground, ignoring the traitor, ignoring the tingling of his touch.

There was an unusual bite in the air as he hauled me down the rocky corridor, but the chill didn't bother me. I felt nothing, barely registering the tears streaming down my pale cheeks.

He made me feel empty.

And I hated him for it.

Hated he had deceived me. Hated he had made me fall in love with him. Hated he had given me hope, a promise of the future. How could I have been so naive, so stupid? He was the very thing I detested, yet my powers had failed me, failed to let me see him for what he truly was.

Lilith's son!

Air left my lungs, as if I'd been sucker punched.

Alone and with Zavier against me, my chances of defeating the vampire queen seemed hopeless. I didn't know how I would escape. How I would find the strength to get through what Lilith had in store for me.

A cold prickle brushed the back of my neck.

"You can hate me all you want, and trust me, I taste your hatred in the air," Zavier muttered.

Good. I wanted him to feel the sting, but it wasn't nearly enough punishment.

As Zavier led me back down the depressing hall, all I could

think about was the deep cut of his betrayal. It was like an open wound to my heart, bleeding in an endless fountain of raw emotions.

The only good I could find in this situation was at least I knew who he was really loyal to. Sure, the bastard broke my heart, and I had probably been kidnapped because of Zavier, but my desire to kill the vampire queen hadn't altered.

The feelings of unease and mistrust that had been there the first week resurfaced. How could I have been so blind? How could I have fallen for someone like him?

I had opened myself up, allowed myself to love him when I had kept my heart so closely guarded, and what had he done? He shattered my trust into a million fragmented pieces, and I refused to think what he had managed to do to my heart.

Had this whole thing been a ploy to get close to me? A plot to infiltrate the compound from the inside? To seduce me, make me care for him?

I was angry all right, but I was more furious with myself.

Pressure clamped down on my chest, and my hands clenched and unclenched at my sides. Given the opportunity, I wouldn't hesitate to do what I had to do, even if going through Zavier was the only way.

I refused to let myself think about our bond, and how the only man I loved was a traitor.

Hell hath no fury like a woman scorned. Zavier was about to find out how deadly I could be.

This place had to be massive maze of turns and tunnels. Even if I managed to kill Lilith, how would I ever find my way out? It seemed as if there was no hope for escape.

As he walked, sounds from within the chambers slowly penetrated through my emotional haze and sent ice racing through my limbs. Voices, cries, and pleas echoed off the mildewed stone walls. This was a prison, humans and witches held against their will.

We turned a corner, and entered yet another corridor. At the end, there was a door. Zavier stepped through, and immediately a sense of recognition washed over me. He set me on my feet, locking the door behind us. I wrapped my arms around myself, forcing one foot in front of the other as I moved further into the room.

It was a place that looked as if it didn't belong underground, much like Lilith's personal chambers. The bed in the center was made of royal-blue silk. It smelled of male, one particular male I'd thought I had known. It brought an upsurge of fresh memories that suddenly felt like years ago, instead of only hours. The lack of windows and natural light gave the area a stuffy and cold vibe. Contained too long down here, I would grow restless, like a caged cat.

"Skylar." Zavier spoke, breaking the silence.

The sound of his deep, smooth voice unleashed something inside me. I spun around, swinging at him a second time.

He was prepared. The half-breed caught my wrist, holding it in the air as his eyes held mine. He whipped me around, intending to box me in with his arms, but I kicked out. He narrowly avoided being kneed in the groin. "Stop this. I won't fight you." Anger churned in the glow of his eyes.

"How could you?" I launched again, claws out, ready to do severe damage to his face. To my frustration, he easily dodged my attack, and I ran into something hard, smacking my head. Two seconds later, I'd barely caught my breath before Zavier grabbed me around the waist, slamming me into the bed. It became a tangle of arms and limbs as I went wild underneath him.

He let out a curse. Managed to secure my wrists over my

head, he trapped me with his body. "You need to calm down before *you* get hurt."

"You mean the knife you jabbed in my back wasn't enough?"

He leaned down so our noses almost touched. "Stop fighting," he growled. "I told you my family was complicated. I wasn't joking. Lilith didn't raise me here. She didn't raise me at all. I was never part of her coven."

"You expect me to believe you?" I hurled.

"So I left out a few tiny details, but can you blame me? If the vampire queen were your mother, would you go around announcing it to the world? Now listen, I am only going to speak of this once. Do you understand?"

I bit my lip, when I really wanted to scream in agony. "I won't listen to anything you have to say."

He sighed. "You will, minx, if you want your revenge and to stop the Bay from another catastrophic event. Together, we can make that happen."

I tilted my chin. "You're insane. I'll never trust you."

"You don't have a choice," Zavier gritted.

I bucked my hips, realizing immediately what a bad idea that was. My body reacted, tingles radiating. Damn him. Damn what he could make me feel. I hated him—wanted to detest him. Forcing my body to go limp, I dropped my head onto the bed. "I'll never forgive you."

"Maybe, but it was a chance I had to take. Your brother—"

"Colin knows," I interrupted, my ears unable to believe what I was hearing. "Of course he does. My brother loves to keep his secrets."

"When they are in the best interest of the city he is sworn to protect, he has little choice," Zavier growled. "This decision wasn't made lightly. He came to me and asked for my help, not only for your protection, but also for the Bay. Colin knew you would never let go of your desire for revenge. He also knew he needed to do something to prevent what the vampire queen has in store."

"Were you ever part of the guard?"

"Yes. Not everything I told you was a lie. Colin and I have known each other for years. I was, in fact, raised by a witch, not by Lilith."

"Get off me." I struggled against the hands holding my wrists. I didn't want to listen to his sad childhood story. I didn't want to feel an ounce of sympathy for the man or the vampire.

His hold on me held. "Do I have your word you won't try anything else stupid?"

I lifted a single brow. "Define stupid."

We both knew I wanted to string him up by his balls. "Sky, that includes hitting me again," he added.

What was the point of lying? "I do want to hit you again, and I doubt the feeling will pass."

Zavier was faster and stronger than me, and if he wanted, he could have me back in the same position in five seconds flat.

"Understandable. And there will come a time when you can act out on those urges, just not today."

My gaze flicked to his smirking lips. Slowly, the feeling to stab him ebbed. "Fine. I'll behave…for the moment."

Knock it off. You have no business thinking about his lips, unless it's to draw blood.

Why did I have to love this half-breed? It wasn't fair. He hurt me in ways he couldn't ever understand.

Zavier let out a ragged breath. Still holding onto my wrists, he helped me up. "I hated lying to you, but I had no choice. I'm not the bad guy."

I snorted, rolling my wrists to put the feeling back into them. "Says the vampire holding me against my will."

"Half," he said, as he was so fond of pointing out every chance he got.

"Where are we?" I asked, noticing this wasn't a cell. My feet touched the cool floor as I glanced around.

"My chambers."

My gaze whipped to his. "Your chambers?" I echoed, the outrage clear. He had a room in Lilith's underground palace. My eyes swept over the room, viewing it with a different perspective. It made sense now why there was a familiarity in the air. The sheets on the bed were ruffled, drawing my eyes, and the last place I wanted to be was alone with Zavier in any room that had a bed.

He raked a hand through his dark hair. "I thought you would be more comfortable."

"And what? Making me comfortable is suddenly a priority?" I edged off the bed and strutted to the door. "Take me back," I demanded, feeling this horrible sinking sense of betrayal.

"No. I get that our relationship is complicated…" he started to say.

I spun around, feeling my hackles go up. "Our relationship is nothing. We *are* nothing! The sooner you get it through your thick skull—"

Whoosh.

He was no longer sitting on the bed, but was standing in front of me, pressing my back against the door with his body. Grabbing my hand, he flipped my arm over. "This mark says we have more than a relationship. You're mine. You will always be mine."

I snatched my wrist from under his fingers. "I don't give a rat's ass what this mark means. Besides, maybe that was part of your plan, to bind me to you."

"You know that is crap. I can't fake the emotions I feel for you."

Damn his stupid voice, the voice that had told me he loved me...

I flinched, biting my lower lip. He might be right. Maybe he couldn't fake his love, but it didn't change the situation. I was still a prisoner. "It doesn't matter, unless you remove these damn shackles from my feet and get me out of here."

"If I could, I would, but I don't have the key," he tried to reason with me.

He wasn't talking about a tangible key. These were magically bound, only broken by a witch. Kind of ironic, since I was a witch, yet couldn't use magic. "Just as I thought. Lies."

"I'm trying to tell you the truth," he insisted, hissing between his teeth.

I angled my head to the side, refusing to shy from the darkness that lived within him. He could flash his fangs all night long, but I wasn't afraid of him. "As if you're capable of doing such a thing."

"Blame me all you want, hate me now if you must, but I know how you truly feel about me, what you can't admit to yourself now." His hand rested over my heart, the fire in his eyes melting. "What I feel for you is very real, as real as the air I breathe."

I wanted to scrape my nails down his pretty face. Was he being serious? Did he expect me to tell him I loved him and all was forgiven? "That's great, but it isn't going to help me or keep me safe. Haven't you hurt me enough?"

He sent me a look I couldn't decipher. "I don't want you hurt, minx, believe it or not. Your safety is still my only concern, which is why I'm here, in a place I vowed never to return."

Don't do it, Sky. Don't let him pull on your heartstrings. I motioned to my ankles. "If you don't want to see me harmed, find a witch to take these off." I tapped my heels together, making the chain links jingle.

"I would, but the moment you're free, how do I know you won't try to incinerate me from the inside out?"

At least he understood me. "No more than you deserve," I spat.

He curled his hand under my arm, helping me stand.

I jerked out of his hold, words of anger spewing from my lips before I could stop them. There was so much hurt and rage built up inside me. I was going to explode if I didn't release it. "Don't ever touch me."

"You like being caged?" he asked.

Coldness radiated over my body. Who was this man? Where was the warden who inspired such a rush of emotions and heat? As I stared into his eyes, I didn't know this vampire in front of me. "You like having two balls?" I countered.

Those lips I used to dream about twitched, now all I wanted to do was punch him. "I'm glad to see you haven't lost your spirit. You're going to need it to get through this ordeal."

No shit, Sherlock. I took a step and wavered, pain shooting through my ankles. I winced.

"Did you hurt yourself?" Zavier's eyes went straight to the shackles. He crouched in front of me, inspecting the cuts caused by the metal. "You're bleeding."

"What do you care?" I snapped. The wounds I received from last night's surprise attack had reopened while I'd made a sad attempt to break free. Blood oozed from the gash on the side of my left ankle. I hissed.

Straightening to his full height, he kept his gaze locked on mine. "Contrary to what you think of me right now, I am your only hope. I want to give you what you desire, minx." His voice was just above a whisper.

I angled my head to the side, wondering what he was getting at. What game was he playing now? "And what is it you think I want? To be a prisoner? To be your sex slave?" I scoffed. As if I would ever let the half-breed put his paws on me again. Mate or not, I would find a way to break our bond.

"Revenge."

He sure knew how to tease a girl. I'd give him that. "I refuse to be duped by you again."

Zavier closed the space between us, hard determination locking his jaw. "No tricks. No lies. I swear it. I want her dead the same as you."

My chin shot up. "How can you possibly expect me to trust you? You're here, in the vampire nest as one of them. I'm not stupid."

"I never thought you were."

"What has the vampire queen done to you? Are you one of her loyal subjects, sent to do her bidding? It is obvious where your devotion lies."

A muscle popped on Zavier's face. "I have my reasons. You forget. I'm only half-vampire."

I hadn't forgotten, but it didn't change my position or how I felt about him. "Why would I believe you? Trust you?"

He shook his head. "The moment I got wind of your abduction, I came immediately. I hurt you by keeping the truth about who I was from you, but it was never what I wanted. I didn't know how strong I would feel about you."

Conflicted feelings of love and anger mingled inside me. "Yeah, that backfired, didn't it?"

He studied me intently, captivating me in the same way I enthralled him. It was strange. Part of me responded with excitement to the intensity of his gaze. "I tried to pretend I felt nothing for you, tried to convince myself you would be safer not mixed up with me, but when I'm near you, all my senses go on high alert. You're the first thing I think about when I wake up, and the last before I fall asleep. I couldn't let you go even if I tried, and now that your soul is linked to mine, there is no turning back time."

"What a lovely speech. How long have you been rehearsing it?" I said dryly.

"I knew this wasn't going to be easy, but you know me, I'm always up for a challenge."

"You still haven't told me what I'm doing here."

A shadow fell across his face in such a way that it made the silver in his eyes hard to see. He didn't inherit the usual iridescent eyes of a vampire. "Lilith has been searching for you for years, for the blood of a Rift witch. She wants more than your power. Don't get me wrong—her sole agenda is to reverse the blood curse—but she also wants something else from you."

"A child," I guessed.

He nodded. "The perfect hybrid, a vampire with the ability to do magic, strong magic."

Knots formed in my belly. The bitch wanted to impregnate me with her son's vampire seed. "Over my dead body. I would never let her near my child."

"That makes two of us." He walked to one of the plush armchairs, folding his six-foot-two frame into the seat.

"Does Colin know I've been taken?"

He nodded. "By now he does."

"Crap," I mumbled.

"Exactly. Colin will have every man alive looking for you around the clock. He won't stop until you're safely at Silent Bend again."

"He must be going crazy."

"I imagine he is. Vampires are not all evil spawns of hell, you know."

"Maybe not to you."

"You have your reasons to hate them. What Lilith took from you is unforgiveable, but for both our lives, I'm going to give you a piece of advice. Don't entice her displeasure. She is even more reckless than you when provoked. She needs you, but that doesn't mean your life isn't in danger. Her impulsiveness can still get you killed."

"I can't make any promises," I replied, keeping my face blank. I took a seat on the edge of bed, keeping the space of the room between us. "If you're really here to help me, how is it I am going to get the chance to kill your mother?"

His lips twisted into a wry smile. "I'm so glad you asked."

Blood would certainly flow, and some of it might be mine.

CHAPTER 22

Crossing my legs, I studied Zavier, trying to make sense out of this mess. It was hard to see him as he had once been to me, a warden with this mysterious aura of invincibility. My gaze flicked to the mark on the inside of his wrist. I was ignoring its twin—the one I also wore. If Colin only knew the disorder I'd made of my life. Big brother couldn't save me this time. "Did Colin agree to this?"

"You being captured? Definitely not. There were things in your brother's plan he hadn't accounted for, like the vampire queen being able to find you as quickly as she did. Invading your dreams was a dirty trick. I got wind of your planned abduction as it was unfolding, and I knew we were going to need an ally inside. I couldn't leave you here alone."

"Wonderful. The world is on the brink of a colossal shit storm, and I'm stuck underground with someone who claims to love me, yet here we are."

Zavier's lips turned into a smile. "Technically, I didn't kidnap you. I'm a double agent who is going to rescue you."

I propped my elbow on my knee, and laid my chin into the

palm of my hand. "Comrade, you might need to step up your game. These shackles on my ankles are starting to piss me off."

"Trust me, I'm working on it. It shouldn't be much longer. Lilith will summon you again. Soon. The vampire queen isn't known for her patience, and now that she has you in her lair, she isn't going to waste time. You aren't the only who has waited years for this moment."

"How is it you weren't raised in her coven, but by a witch?" I asked, curious despite myself.

"I was different. She only saw the human in me, not the vampire heir she wanted. A witch found me in the woods."

I raised a brow. "She abandoned you as a baby?"

He nodded, standing up and pacing the room. "I have no loyalty to Lilith, and the only reason I am allowed in her coven is because of you, not because she trusts me."

The woman wasn't fit to raise a child. I would drop dead before I let her anywhere near mine. "She means to use our child, but why?"

His eyes flicked from my face to my stomach and back. "Are you?"

I made a face and shook my head. "No. I made sure I was protected." Birth control wasn't an option in the Bay, unless people sought a witch for a potion or a spell. I happened to take care of my own birth control, by the rune etched into my inner thigh.

He exhaled, the panic lines that had crinkled at the edges of his eyes relaxing. "Good, because you're right, she would use that child to get us to do what she wants. Lilith has witches in her possession, but they've stopped being able to sire vampires, and none of them have the amount of power required to reverse the curse. Her line is dwindling. Each time she sends a group out into the Bay in search of a witch, she risks losing members of the coven."

"And the human babies who have been born, what does she do with them?" I was almost afraid to ask.

"What do you think? There hasn't been an abundance of infants in the village."

My eyes widened. "S-she kills them."

"They are useless to her."

I shuddered, wrapping my arms around myself. "I'm going to rip out her dead heart."

"Brave words, little minx."

"They're true," I replied defiantly. "You know that the first chance I get, I will kill her." Not just for my mom, but for every innocent she had taken from this world.

He sat on the bed beside me, his weight dipping the foam mattress. His scent drifted in the air, and my heart skipped. "You've the blood of a Rift witch. Your power is stronger than any other in the Bay. You might be the only person who can defeat her."

"You won't stand in my way?"

Without warning, he reached out and ran his fingers along the side of my face. I gasped, remembering the way he touched me, and it was the same now, exactly as I remembered. "I will stand beside you. She can no longer keep poisoning the Bay with her madness. I won't let her take what is mine."

I swallowed. He meant me. I wanted to trust him, and through the connection I didn't want, I could tell he believed in the words he was saying. "How much time do we have?" Lilith wasn't a patient vampire. She would summon me again, and soon. We both knew it.

"Not long enough." He caught hold of my hand, placing it

over his chest. "No matter what you think of me, this is real, what I feel for you is real. I would give my life to keep you safe."

I froze, and stopped breathing altogether. "I can't think about that now." Feelings muddled the brain, and I needed my wits if I was going to stay alive.

Both of his hands moved up and cupped my face. His fingertips were light. "After then, when you get your justice, we're going to talk." A finger trailed down the side of my neck, coming to rest on the pulsing vein. Heat leapt into his eyes, implying he wanted to do more than talk to me.

I stared at him, memories of his fangs sinking blissfully into my neck making their way into the forefront of my mind, and once there, I couldn't stop thinking about how it had felt. "Assuming we make it out of here alive."

"There's that little tidbit, and in the meantime, you should try to get some sleep. You're going to need your strength to get us through what comes next. Whatever that may be."

He was right, but how could I close my eyes and relax in the place of my archenemy? With my head on the bed, I thought about extracting my revenge on Lilith. Never in a million years had I envisioned it like this. How had I gotten so derailed from my path?

۞

I DIDN'T DREAM that night. I dropped into a void of sleep, floating there until my body had enough.

As I stirred and began to wake, a child's face appeared in my mind. She had the face of angel, rosy cheeks, raven hair, and eyes that twinkled like stars in a moonless night. The beautiful baby's face blurred with Lilith's.

She was poised on her black throne, tapping her long, dark nails with impatience. "Bring her to me," she demanded.

I tucked the baby underneath my cloak, as if that would keep her safe. "I'll bring this cavern down on our heads before I let you anywhere near her."

Lilith didn't flinch. She was unmoved by my threats, so confident in her authority. "And risk the baby's life? I think not." She smirked, calling my bluff.

Before I had a chance to do anything, I was sandwiched by two vampires. A scream wrenched from my lungs as I tried to turn to protect my child. My scream turned to pure terror as the baby was ripped from my arms, her soft cries piercing my heart.

I bolted up, fear rising in my throat like acidic bile. The little girl had been mine, I was sure of it, and Lilith had taken her—my daughter. My fingers bunched on the bed, nails digging into my skin.

Disorientated, I blinked, forgetting where I was until I moved my feet and heard the clanking of the chains around my feet. *Lilith*, my mind hissed. The large bed was silky and rumpled.

And then I remembered. My magic didn't work here. The shackles stripped me of my power, of any defense I might have against the vampires. I exhaled in an attempt to calm my pounding heart.

"What is it?" Zavier asked in the darkened room.

I heard his voice, but the bed beside me was empty. My eyes scanned the room until they landed on my mate. He was sitting near the simmering fire. "Just a dream." There was no sense in worrying him when I didn't know if any of it was true. I couldn't possibly pregnant, and if I was, Lilith couldn't know. It was far too soon. Conception took time for detection, and I planned to kill the vampire queen before she ever got the chance to hope. "What time is it?" I asked.

His head lifted. "Dawn."

I wasn't going to ask if he had slept, for I already knew the answer. He had watched over me. "She's coming for me."

"She will, but you're safe for now," he assured me, standing and walking over to the bed.

I grabbed his hand, and clung to his coolness. "She is done waiting. She wants the blood curse reversed tonight." I was putting a lot into trusting Zavier, and if it wasn't for this bond between us, I wasn't sure I would have been able to go further into the vampire's nest.

A knock sounded.

My body tensed as I stood up, and I glanced at Zavier one last time. He might not have been the man I thought he was, or the man I saw myself falling in love with, but faced with death, I was glad it was him. There were many regrets in my life, but I found that being Zavier's mate was not one of them.

CHAPTER 23

Zavier hauled me against his chest, kissing me soundly. It was a kiss to remember, and that was exactly his intent.

"Don't make me tear this door down," came a voice from the other side of the door.

Zavier brushed his lips along my cheek. "Know that whatever happens, I love you, minx." Then he strutted across the room, and whipped open the door. No surprise. It was Aeron.

The vampire darkened the doorway, hatred etched onto his beautiful features. Or fury. It was hard to tell. There was very little similarity between the brothers. "Mummy calls," Aeron announced.

Zavier grimaced. "Give me five."

"Now!" Aeron demanded, fangs extending to their full limit. "You know how she hates to be kept waiting. Besides, if you haven't gotten her in bed yet, then you might need to work on your game, bro."

Zavier's expression hardened. "We're not bros."

"Our DNA says otherwise," Aeron was quick to point out.

Zavier covertly stepped in front of me. "I don't give a flying fuck about shared genetic makeup. Let's get this over with so I can get back to my life."

"*If* she allows it."

The brothers stared at each other, each of equal height, but Aeron didn't have the broad build Zavier did. He was lanky. "Just stay out of my way, and there won't be any problems," Zavier warned.

"You think you have us fooled, but I can taste your desire to protect the witch. If you stand in Lilith's way, you'll both end up dead."

"We'll see," Zavier seethed, slipping a hand to the small of my back and ushering me through the door.

A cold prickle brushed the back of my neck, but I didn't dare glance over my shoulder. One moment of distraction could cost me my life if Aeron decided to chop off my head.

I was led into a cavern similar to the one from yesterday. At least, I thought it had only been twenty-four hours, but it was impossible to tell. This chamber was different in that it had a witch's touch. In the center of the room, a circle was carved into the ground, and the air was tinged with burning candle wax.

Lilith stood in the center, looking bored and put out. Her hair was a perfect river of black flowing over her milky shoulders. Her lips twisted into a parody of a smile. "We have unfinished business. Now that you've had time to reflect on what is at stake, I assume you're ready to give me what I want."

Zavier and Aeron flanked either side of me in case I got any funny ideas. "You know what they say about assuming?"

Lilith didn't have much of a sense a humor, and she was

short on patience. "I'm going to reverse the blood spell with or without your submission," she hissed.

My spine stiffened. "Are you demented? There is no way I am performing that spell. Your little circle of witches is going to have to execute it without me." I didn't even know a spell that could do such a thing, but my guess was that Lilith had spent years researching how it could be done.

"I'm pretty sure we already established my evil badges. You either do the spell or people die. Is that clear enough for you? And in case you need additional motivation, I'll start the killing spree with your mate." Her lips twisted. "This would be so much less bloody if you did the spell willingly, not that I am against a little spilled blood."

I tried to swallow the lump in my throat. "You'd kill your own son?"

"I'd like to see you try." Rage deepened Zavier's voice, his eyes flaring brilliant silver.

I wanted to call her bluff, but looking at the vampire queen, I realized she would do it. She would kill her own son. "I can't allow you to reverse the spell," I gritted.

"It is admirable the lengths you would go to protect your people. You can understand my desire to do the same. If we don't reverse the curse, my kind will fall into extinction. Traditional methods of conceiving are failing, and we are left without any insurances. What would you do in my position?"

Not kill my own son. "You chose to enslave witches. Force them against their will to bear children instead of coming to the council for a solution."

She threw back her head and laughed. "The council is a joke. You must see those old fools no nothing of the future. They are too stuck on the past."

There was no way I was going to give her what she

wanted, but it didn't hurt to play with the vampire a bit. Heck, I might even get lucky and get these shackles off. Then she really wouldn't like me much. "If you want me to reverse the spell, you're going to need to take these off me." I jingled the chains at my feet. "I need my mojo."

Lilith's chuckle was edged with bitterness. "I'm not a fool. All in good time."

I stepped forward, invading the vampire's personal space. "You should have killed me when you had the chance."

Her eyes brightened, glowing in the dark space. "Who says I still won't? Or would you rather suffer an eternity of endless torment? I can make that happen."

"From one crazy bitch to another, screw off," I snapped, forcing my feet to stay planted.

Lilith hissed, her elongated fangs proving she wasn't someone to be trifled with. "You've sealed your fate and your mate's." She grabbed my chin between her fingers. "Tatiana, cast the spell while I give our little witch a taste of her future," Lilith commanded as she increased the pressure of her grip.

I refused to flinch.

A slim figure emerged from the shadows, and I stared in fear and fascination. Such cloaking could only be magic. This was the witch who had been aiding Lilith. Her power was strong. I sensed it trembling in the air around her as she stepped into the circle etched into the rocky floor.

Shit.

"I did warn you the spell would commence regardless of your willingness. Tatiana will channel your powers, while I teach you a lesson." She released my chin with a force that sent me stumbling, her focus on Zavier.

"Sky, get out of here," Zavier barked, claws and fangs extending as he went into vamp-mode.

I gritted my teeth. He was insane if he thought I was going to leave him alone to fight both his delusion mother and psychotic brother, but to be any assistance, I needed my power.

Turning, I planted myself squarely in front of the witch Tatiana. "Where do you think you're going?"

The witch's almond-shaped eyes were huge, trembling with fright. "You don't understand. I don't have a choice."

I cursed the binds at my feet. "And neither do I. Remove these shackles. Now! I won't ask a second time."

Behind me, I heard the ghastly sounds of claws tearing into flesh, followed by grunts of pain and bones snapping. I didn't turn to watch the battle, but took strength from my certainty Zavier was still alive. How else could I feel the warden's emotions?

I had hoped intimidation would work on the frightened witch. No such luck. She shook her head, eyes darting all over the place. "I can't. She'll kill me. I've seen what she does to witches who disobey her. If you knew what was wise, you would do the spell."

"You mean what *you've* helped her do. She wouldn't have been able to locate all those witches without *your* power," I not so nicely pointed out.

"Don't move," she warned as I took a step closer.

Maybe I could tackle her to the ground if I got close enough. "There's no escape, no magic door, no fairy godmother. We need each other if either of us have a chance of surviving."

A short, almost hysterical laugh escaped Tatiana. "We both know there is no chance either of us are walking away from this. If there is one thing I've learned, it's that no one who enters her lair leaves alive."

A frightening thought, however true, but I was looking at the bigger picture, even if it meant my own life. "If you do this, you'll be destroying Division Fourteen. Is that what you want?"

"Not everyone will be destroyed."

She meant vampires. "You can't be that stupid." I didn't have time to argue with the witch. "The way I see it, either way you die. Free me so we can at least give the Bay a chance to be saved, protect those we still love."

Her eyes dashed toward the fight behind me. Zavier was doing a bitchin' job giving me time, but I knew I had only seconds left. The witch's face paled, her gaze returning to me. "I'm sorry, but I'm going to siphon your power. It's the only way."

The hell she was. I was desperate, which meant it was time for drastic measures. I bum-rushed her, taking us both to the ground, and lucky for me, I had the cushion of her body to soften my landing. Using my weight to keep her pinned to the floor, I rammed my forearm into her throat. "I'm going to ask you one more time. Undo the spell on these shackles or I'll snap your neck."

Tatiana stared into my eyes, and there was so much weariness. "You've just issued both our death sentences." She closed her eyes, whispering a chant.

The shackles broke away, giving me more than my freedom. My power was back. It was sweeter than sex. Well, almost. "I guess we'll find out." I sprang to my feet, my only concern stopping Lilith.

My gaze automatically landed on Zavier, who was cornered by his brother and another vampire. There was a bit of blood on his face, but at least he wasn't dead. My eyes darted around the cavern, looking for the queen bitch. "Come out, come out, wherever you are," I muttered.

"Ding, dong, the witch is dead," Lilith said in a patronizing tone.

My spine stiffened, and I spun around. She was holding Tatiana by her hair. The witch's body hung lifeless, her eyes vacant, blood dripping from her mouth. The stark reality of Tatiana's final words rang through my head. I had issued her death warrant. A violent and powerful surge of power trembled through my veins. "You'll pay for that, and all the other lives you stole. Too bad my mother hadn't delivered you to hell instead of trying to save you."

Lilith dropped Tatiana to the ground as if her life had less meaning than a pesky fly. "And there it is. The reason why you're exactly the witch I need. You aren't your mother. I have no doubt you would have no qualm over killing me."

I squeezed my fingers into my palms as my stomach dropped for the witch I couldn't protect. Maybe I was the fool. "My mother was a good person," I said, anguish leaking into my words.

The vampire halted, angling her head to one side. "And you're not." Her mocking gaze flicked over my face. "Ridiculous girl. I am not going to be thwarted by a witch." Her attention shifted to Zavier. "Or the half-breed with my blood. You don't believe I thought you were here for me?" she spat at Zavier.

He had broken off from his fight, the body of one of Lilith's vampire guards discarded in his wake. Standing on the other side of his mother, stake in his grasp, he spread his feet in a fighter stance, prepared for an attack.

My anger jumped to fear. The vision I had earlier came back to haunt me. There might be worse things than death—

my child in the hands of someone like her. I couldn't let that happen. There was no future for any of us if I didn't stop her here and now.

"It was I who took her, and it was I who took you. Her daughter and my son." She sneered. "What poetic justice. The power of her magic took what made us vampires, and you will give it back to us."

Over my scrawny bootie. "How many times do I have to tell you that is never going to happen?" I spat. Lightning snapped from the sky.

Throwing back her raven head, she laughed, the sound of a seductress. "Everyone has a price. And I know yours."

My eyes frantically searched her for deceit. It was so hard for me to believe she would kill her own flesh and blood, but it was there in her eyes, hard as glass. The bitch didn't have a heart.

I raised my hand, intending to activate one of the runes on my body, but before I could touch the mark, a scream strangled my throat as I was slammed against the wall.

Wildly, I tried to struggle against the grasp that held me pressed to the side of the cavern. Distantly, I was aware Zavier was rushing toward me, but he didn't get far.

Vampires surrounded him. I had to decide, but faced with Zavier's blood on my hands, faced with losing the only man I had ever loved, I found I couldn't let Lilith hurt him.

Could I give up my revenge to save him?

Lilith's lips twisted in a smirk that shone with victory. "Shall we begin?"

I stayed tightlipped, my mind whirling.

As if I needed more incentive, Aeron stepped up to his brother, but the bastard kept his eyes on me. His fangs gleamed as the corners of his lips lifted. Extending his hand,

Aeron flicked out a sharpened claw while three other vampires kept Zavier prisoned. "This won't hurt much," Aeron told him with immense pleasure.

"Go to hell," Zavier growled.

"Where do you think I've been?" Aeron retorted. With a savagely quick swipe, he dragged his razor-sharp nail down the side of Zavier's neck.

At the first sight of his blood, the roaring fear rushed like a broken dam inside me, and I made a hasty choice. "Don't!" I yelled. "I'll give you what you want. I'll reverse the curse. But only under the condition you let him go."

Victory lit the bitch queen's face. "Finally, you're making sense."

"Skylar," Zavier rumbled.

"What?" I snapped. "Do you expect me to let her kill you? I could still change my mind, you know."

"Don't do this," he warned.

"This is your fault, you know. If you hadn't made me fall in love with you, I wouldn't care what happens to you."

Lilith's laughter brushed over my skin with a biting chill. "At last, I shall have back what was taken from me."

"Oh, you're definitely going to get what you deserve." I couldn't overpower the vampire even with all my training, but I could damn well make her regret hurting what was mine.

I stumbled backward, my heart frozen in my chest. Victory was etched into Lilith's beautiful face, but her beauty was all a lie. I knew what she looked like deep in her soul. She was filled with nothing but greed, hunger, and selfishness. She cared for no one but herself. Certainly not the Bay or the people who lived in it.

Zavier deserved a mother who was a thousand times the vampire she was.

She flashed in front of me, her lips brushing over mine, and they were cold, bitter cold. My heart began to beat hard and fast in my chest. "Did you sleep well, little witch? I had the most interesting dream—a child—a little girl with hair as dark as a raven and sparkling eyes like a thousand stars in a moonless sky."

"You bitch," I seethed, my chin tilting up. "Stay the hell out of my head."

She smiled, the white of her fangs gleaming against the dreadful night. "I've been called by many names; however, magnificent has always been a personal favorite. I'm magnificent, and so will you be, once you give me what I want."

"I will paint the earth with your blood, Lilith."

"You can try, my dear, but first you will do the spell."

My heart was jackhammering in my chest, realizing she knew I would have a child, Zavier's child, and what she planned to do with the knowledge turned my blood to ice.

Lilith shoved me to the ground in the center of the circle, my knees cracking against the stone. "Time is a ticking. How long do you think your lover has before he is drained of blood?"

The eyes of the vampires surrounding Zavier had all gone dark at the sight of his blood dripping down his throat. "I'm sorry," I mouthed.

"Skylar!" Zavier hollered.

"Summon your power," Lilith demanded. "Channel your coven."

"I don't have a choice," I whispered, hoping Zavier would understand. He might not have the gift of sight, but he was going to have to trust me in this.

My palms flattened over the stone, and I closed my eyes, concentrating on the pulse of magic at my core. Tears stung my eyes as I chanted the words that would bring darkness inside me. There were two types of power in this world—black and white—dark and good. Often, black magic was stronger, and although I'd never dabbled in the dark side, I was willing to battle in the filth if it meant I could defeat the vampire once and for all.

The consequences would be dealt with later, for there was always a price for magic. I would gladly take the scars for the greater good, or so I reasoned for my desperate actions. It clawed and slashed inside me, the air flashing with a heaviness of pressure ready to unleash.

This was the kind of magic Lilith demanded to remove the blood curse, but I'd rather send her to hell. As my lungs labored and my heart pounded, I ignored the warnings rumbling in my head.

I was power now. Beyond anything I'd ever felt.

Lilith grabbed a handful of my hair, yanking my head back. "What did you do?"

"Let me show you." A scream was wrenched from my throat as I used my power to slam Aeron against the wall. The blast knocked back the other guards, giving Zavier an opening.

He didn't hesitate, baring his fangs and pressing them to Aeron's throat. Zavier thrust the stake into the other vampire's chest. "Goodbye, brother."

With a growl, Aeron reared back. Shock and pain rushed over his face for instant, his hand clutching the wound on his chest. Aeron fell. Zavier had killed the vampire queen's devoted son and heir.

Lilith's scream was that of pure rage.

CHAPTER 24

T he time has come. I am going to kill her.

A boost of adrenaline pumped through my body, joining the surge of magic. I would bring down the cave walls around me if that was what it took to stop her. Faint sparks of magic glittered over my skin, the power intensifying and growing with every heartbeat.

Lilith's hand streaked out, her nails raking down my cheek. "You think you can defeat me?" she hissed, licking the blood from her fingers. "A hundred cuts. That's what I'll give you each time you defy me." Her slim hand curled around my neck.

Her fingers tightened, cutting off my air supply. At the direct threat on my life, my powers struck out. Lilith cursed, releasing her grasp and taking a step in retreat. I struggled to keep my balance as I sucked in a breath of air.

Lilith's furious eyes glanced down at her hand, fangs extending when she saw the blackened flesh, burned and shriveled. I had managed to do more damage than I'd expected.

Fury rocked her body, her eyes smoldering with hate. She struck, her fangs piercing my flesh. I heard my own scream. It was in the madness of pain and heat so hot the burn was unspeakable, through my skin and into my blood.

Her hand lifted high in the air, poised to strike, but she wasn't the only one with strong emotions. Using all my grief and rage, I struck at her with open palms, calling forth the surge of magic flowing in my veins without considering the consequences.

She flew back in the air, twisting and shrieking as lightning rippled through the darkness.

"Skylar!" Zavier called. He was leaning against the rocky wall, his hand pressed to his neck, covered in his own blood. I could see he was weakening, and wouldn't be able to hold his own against Lilith's guards for long.

This needed to end. Now.

Lilith was skilled, but I'd expected nothing less. She didn't become the vampire she was by being lazy.

Recovering with incredible speed, the vampire queen landed on her feet and came charging toward me, slamming me into a wall. "You little bitch, I could have given you power beyond your dreams. I am going to take my time killing you." Her hand swung out, striking like a deadly cobra as she raked her nails down my other cheek.

I tasted blood in my mouth, and there was more seeping out of the dozen shallow slices on my skin. I knew that I had wounded her, but not enough to render the bitch dead. My own power was ebbing out. "You need me. We both know it. There isn't another descendant of a Rift witch in the Bay."

"Isn't there?" she challenged with superior smugness. "Maybe not one as strong as you, but your brother is still a witch."

I glared at Lilith, wishing I had the strength left to rip out her black heart. Or at the very least, break her perfect nose. All sane thoughts had left my brain the second she mentioned Colin. Curling up my hand, I punched the vile bitch directly in the face.

There was a satisfying crunch and a spurt of blood, but it was an action that would get little result. It didn't matter. It had felt good to give into the urge to hit her. I wanted to do it again and again. "My brother renounced his powers. He is of no use to you."

"Your little outburst makes me think otherwise." Her retaliation was going to hurt. Sharp nails sliced down my chest, cutting through the thin material of my shirt and down my stomach. My cry of torment bounced around the cavern as my blood colored the fabric, staining it a dark crimson.

"If you continue to fight me, I will make your death a slow and agonizing process." Her fingers dug into my hair, pulling my head back as she forced me to look at Zavier. "I can't decide who should die first. You or my traitorous, impure son."

Zavier fought against the vampires who held him, regardless that each movement caused him pain, caused his wound to seep more blood.

I shook my head, gritting my teeth against the pain. I could almost hear Zavier's voice in my head, telling me to fight, to give up, or be swayed by her threats.

Blood was dripping down my body from my wounds, my power was wavering, and I'd be on my knees before long. I needed to strike quickly or I'd have wasted my only opportunity.

Lilith circled around me, her dress dragging over the bloody ground. "Your fire is cooling, little witch."

I lifted my chin in defiance. "I'll destroy you," I gasped out the words. *She'd bleed*. I would saturate the ground with her blood. "I swear it."

"You believe you can, which I find commendable. But that is not how it is foretold. You will fall, one by one. You, Zavier, your brother, his little pack of wardens, and with each death, my power grows. Nothing will stop me, certainly not you."

"I will." Bloody and battered, Zavier struck out with a wooden stake.

She moved so fast, that eerie speed my eyes couldn't follow just blurs of colors. This was my battle, but Zavier wouldn't leave me to fight alone, even against his own blood. He would fight alongside me until his dying breath.

What a guy.

I was only sorry it took until this moment for me to realize he truly only had my well-being in mind, regardless of the secrets and lies. He loved me.

Lilith's hand shot out, clasping onto Zavier's wrist before he could bury the stake in her heart. "Come to save your whore?" Her eyes glistened like frost sparkling in the sun. "Tell me, *son*…" Lilith licked a drop of blood off the side of her lip. It could have been hers, mine, Zavier's, her dead son's—there was so much blood flying about. "Does all this blood stir your desires? I know the vampire in you wants it. I put the hunger in you, and I know the pull, it still lives within me. It is the basis of our life."

"You never knew me," Zavier growled, struggling to over-power the vampire.

Lilith was older, stronger, and more skilled. She had decades to refine the art of being a heartless warrior bitch. Zavier knew it, too. Taking advantage of his weakened state,

Lilith twisted the stake with a force that sent Zavier staggering back…and left her with a weapon to kill him.

"No!" I screamed, lunging forward.

Lilith hissed in satisfaction, baring her fangs. "You can't fight evil with evil."

She was right. This whole time, I'd been consumed with hate. Killing her for selfish reasons, to avenge my mother, but I could no longer think about only myself. I had to defeat Lilith for my future, for Frisco Bay, for Zavier, for Collin, and for Abbey. There was only one way I knew how to do that, and I couldn't do it alone.

Magic.

No beginning.

No end.

A circle—my circle.

I needed them. That was the one thing Lilith lacked. Friends who could be counted on—friends who had one's back through the good, the bad, and the ugly. The connection I had with my circle would allow me to draw the power I needed to defeat her.

Closing a trembling hand around the stone at my neck, I focused all my power into it, and to the witches who had stood beside me. "Power of the elements, power forged by trust, magic, and love, grant my desire, open our minds to the magic of the moon." As I chanted, the air surrounding me shimmered.

The charm flared under my touch, its warmth and light spreading down my arm. I called for Jenna, Bailey, and Raine. This was the only weapon I had. I only hoped that even though our circle wasn't complete, our power would be enough.

Like a river, the tingle of magic flowed down my arms to

my fingertips—my power. It came naturally. The circle on the floor trembled under my feet, and the blood spilled on the cavern floor gathered along the rim, completing the circle around me. Time ticked on in my quest to reach out, but I couldn't feel them, and I began to panic. *Damn it. This hadn't been part of our plan. Was it possible the cave walls were blocking my summoning spell?*

My shoulders began to sag, a sense of hopelessness leaking its way through my grim determination. My heart faltered. Any moment, Lilith was going to expect something magical to happen. She was going to be sorely disappointed. And Zavier and I would probably be too dead to care.

I steeled myself, wracking my brain for my next move. Risking my own life to kill Lilith was something I was okay with, but Zavier's life was another matter. If I failed, life in the Bay we'd rebuilt brick by brick would come crumbling down around us.

And that was when I heard their voices in my head, a familiar chorus of chanting. My head fell back as the surge of power, bright as silver, pumped through my blood. Sucking in a sharp breath, I savored the potency, and the power Jenna, Bailey, and Raine willingly gave to me.

My skin glowed like moonlight, my eyes as dark as stars. Lifting my head and raising my arms, I faced Lilith, feeling indestructible. *Come at me now.*

Lilith smiled. "Finally. Yes, this is what I've waited for, the power I've been searching for."

Good. It was going to be what killed her.

I tossed out my hand, beckoning the discarded wooden stake on the floor. It wobbled once before flying straight into my clutches. As it touched my fingers, it began to glow a brilliant gold, humming and thirsting for a target. Compressing my grasp against the grain of the stake, I steadied my hold, waiting for an opening.

I sliced out, scoring the flesh on her arm. Her rage rang out as blood welled at the wound, black and goopy as slime. She came at me with renewed strength, fury clouding her moments.

"It is I who will destroy you, for the heart of mankind and the purity of magic you can never understand. Rot in hell, queen of the damned," I shouted, lifting my hands over my head. White flames licked from the stake to strike Lilith in the heart like a sword.

Disbelief rushed over her face, her eyes wide, fading, before she lit up like a Christmas tree. Where she dropped and combusted, the ground turned black, ash piling at my feet.

I followed shortly, unable to hold onto consciousness any longer, knowing I finally got the justice I'd dreamed about for so long.

CHAPTER 25

I opened my eyes, and then blinked at the sparkle of silver until Zavier's face came into focus. "Auntie Em?" I croaked, hiding the grin that wanted to curl on my lips.

"Christ," Zavier swore, dragging a hand through his ruffled hair. "Skylar, you better be joking."

"Who's Skylar?" I asked, but couldn't keep up the charade. I started laughing.

His gaze roamed over my face, the shadow of hair on his chin told me I'd been out for hours. "Good one. For two seconds, you scared the shit out of me."

"I'm sure it won't be the last time that happens." I took a moment to see where I was, if we were still in the vampire nest. I wasn't sure how he had managed to get us out, but I was back at the compound, in my own room, tucked into bed. I sighed, content to stay here forever.

My gaze was drawn to the curtains hanging on the open terrace that carried in the hints of sea and forest. The ruby pendant that had been my mother's sat nestled under the twinkle of the nightstand lamp, reminding me of Christmas, maple trees in autumn, and the fancy dinner parties held downstairs.

I was so glad to be home.

I had spent so many years running away, sneaking out, feeling caged, and now I never wanted to leave.

Zavier shifted on the edge of the bed, but even there, his bulky frame took up half the space, his leg brushing against my arm. "Before your mind jumps to all kinds of crazy assumptions, your brother and an army large enough to flatten Lilith's tunnels arrived to safely escort you home."

I blinked, focusing on his face. "She's really dead?"

He nodded. "She is. You killed her. Your revenge has been conquered."

I closed my eyes for a moment, waiting for the burning anger that was always present in my gut, but for the first time in many years, there was peace. And hope.

It was a strange feeling, and I wasn't sure what to do with it.

Zavier's hands drifted over my arm. When it reached my wrist, he flipped my hand over before bringing my arm up to his lips. "I love you," he murmured, his lips brushing over my skin and the mark of our bond. "And I will spend the rest of my life making sure you never doubt it again."

"Good, because I'm not letting you out of my sight, comrade."

"Does this mean you're no longer mad at me?"

"I wouldn't go that far, but it doesn't change that I love you."

His eyes closed as if he were savoring the sound of the three little words I hadn't said to a single man other than my brother and father. "Say it again."

My grin widened, and I intertwined our fingers. "I love you, Zavier Cross, half-vampire and all."

He leaned down and claimed my lips in a kiss of pure possession.

Mine, I swore his voice whispered in my head.

Lilith, the vampire queen, might be dead, but her opulent den remained intact. Well, mostly intact. I wasn't sure how much wreckage Colin's wardens had caused, but I was sure it wasn't enough to wipe away every smear Lilith had left stained on this earth.

There was still work to do, a treaty to uphold, law to enforce, but I would leave all that to my brother. I had done what I set out to do, and now, I was going to live for me, for my child, and for the man who had managed to steal my heart.

Nine months *later*

ॐ

A quiet fog blanketed the Bay. The morning sunlight peeked through, glinting off the dewy blades of dark green grass. Moisture scented the air from the ocean waves crashing against the bluffs. A gentle breeze blew over my legs, and I smiled, happiness I never imagine bursting inside me.

Zavier lifted the infant out of my arms. "She grows prettier every day," he whispered, pressing a gentle kiss to her head.

"I could spend hours just looking at her," I said, nuzzling her soft head, inhaling her innocent baby scent, like soft rose petals and sunshine.

"It is impossible to believe she is ours. To think, I almost lost you both," Zavier said, holding his daughter like a prized possession, loving shining in his eyes.

I rested my chin on his shoulder. "You saved us. When we met, there was only one thing on my mind…getting my revenge. And you did something no else could. You gave me more than peace and justice. You loved me even when I thought you had betrayed me, when I hated you."

His grin was pure male. "I love you with a fierceness that scares me at times."

Love flooded within me as I met his starry gaze. He was my bridge and anchor, this half-vampire warrior. I loved him, truly. My heart opened, and I let the emotions surround me in golden warmth. Love no longer scared me.

What I hadn't known, what I failed to see the night I killed Lilith, was I had already been carrying his child. The vision could have been reality had I not killed Lilith.

I had once burned with hatred for vampires, yearned for nothing more than to wipe them from existence, but now having a half-vampire for a mate and a quarter one for a daughter, I wanted nothing more than to protect them.

Zavier had been right. The ancient tides had awakened. Change was in the air—the signal for a new era was on the horizon.

Hands linked, we walked in the softening sunlight, our sweet baby resting on her father's shoulder. She was our future. And the truest magic was what was in our hearts.

🐾

The End

Thank you for reading.

xoxo

Jennifer

P.S. Join my VIP Readers email list and receive a bonus scene told from Zane's POV, as well as a free copy of Saving Angel, book one in the Bestselling Divisa Series. You will also get notifications of what's new, giveaways, and new releases.

Visit here to sign up: www.jlweil.com

Don't forget to also join my Dark Divas FB Group and have some fun with me and a fabulous, fun group of readers. There is games, prizes, and lots of book love.

Join here:

https://www.facebook.com/groups/1217984804898988/

You can stop in and say hi to me on Facebook night and day. I pop in as often as I can:

https://www.facebook.com/jenniferlweil/ I'd love to hear from you.

READ MORE BY J.L. WEIL

THE DIVISA SERIES

(Full series completed – Teen Paranormal Romance)

Losing Emma: A Divisa novella

Saving Angel

Hunting Angel

Breaking Emma: A Divisa novella

Chasing Angel

Loving Angel

Redeeming Angel

LUMINESCENCE TRILOGY

(Full series completed – Teen Paranormal Romance)

Luminescence

Amethyst Tears

Moondust

Darkmist – A Luminescence novella

RAVEN SERIES

(Full series completed – Teen Paranormal Romance)

White Raven

Black Crow

Soul Symmetry

BEAUTY NEVER DIES

(Teen Dystopian Romance)

Slumber

Entangled

NINE TAILS SERIES

(Teen Paranormal Romance Short Novels)

First Shift

SINGLE NOVELS

Starbound (Teen Paranormal Romance)

Casting Dreams (New Adult Paranormal Romance)

Dark Souls (Runes Series KindleWorld Novella)

Ancient Tides (New Adult Paranormal Romance)

For an updated list of my books, please visit my website:
www.jlweil.com

Join my VIP email list and I'll personally send you an email reminder
as soon as my next book is out! Click here to sign up: www.jlweil.com

A GLIMPSE INSIDE FIRST SHIFT

BOOK ONE IN THE NINE TAILS SERIES

CHAPTER ONE

Two months. Forty-two days to be exact. That was how many days I had left until I graduated from high school and got out of Washington. Not that I was counting or anything.

I slammed my locker shut and spun around, slinging my

backpack stuffed with twenty pounds of books over my back. My friend Hannah talked nonstop, babbling on and on about her weekend plans, but my mind was on the hundred other things I had to do before the day was over. *Forty-two days,* I reminded myself.

"You coming to the game tonight?" Hannah asked.

"I can't. I'm working."

Hannah's cornflower blue eyes sparkled with excitement. "Come on, K. You work too much. You deserve a little fun."

And Hannah Tisdale knew all about fun. She didn't have any responsibilities, didn't know what it was like to have to work hard for everything. Still, she'd been my best friend since third grade. We couldn't be more opposite. Hannah was blonde with big boobs and a big personality to match, yet we somehow complemented each other, rather than clashed. "Fun is a luxury I don't have time for." I checked my watch. "I've got to go."

She followed me, matching my hurried strides. "Please? Please, K? Don't leave me hanging."

"Take Jesse with you," I suggested, giving her a way to go to the game without me as her sidekick.

She rolled her pretty eyes that made most guys do double-takes. "He's on the team. Besides, it's not nearly as fun ogling the lacrosse team's ass cheeks without you," she pouted.

I smiled. "I imagine not."

"Speaking of Jesse. When are the two of you going to admit you have the hots for each other and get it on?"

This time, I rolled my eyes. "He's one of my best friends, Hannah. *Our* best friend," I reminded her. Jesse Hart and I had been neighbors since diapers. Our parents were friends. We hung out all the time and went on family vacations together. I loved him, just not in the way Hannah was constantly suggesting … or so I told myself.

Truthfully, I wasn't sure if I felt something more for Jesse. My life was chaotic right now. There wasn't time for me to think about feelings. With everything going on at home, school, and at the café, I barely had time eat and sleep, let alone dwell on boys.

"You could call in sick. No one at the café would even question it. I mean, when was the last time you took a day off? Or you could say you hit a deer." Melodramatic should have been Hannah's middle name, which made her perfect for drama club. She could think up a hundred different lies without batting an eye.

"But I'm not sick. Nor do I want to hit anything with my car. And I really need the money." I countered her idea, walking out the double doors of Seaside Heights High School.

Hannah scrunched her nose and stopped at the curb. "I'm not changing your mind, am I?"

We'd reached the parking lot. I turned around and walked backwards down the curb. "Nope. Text me later."

Hannah made a face, and I knew what she was thinking: that I work too hard and needed a life outside of school. What was wrong with wanting to get good grades so I could go to college somewhere far, far away from this small, coastal, Washington town? I'd rather be inside studying than stuck at some lacrosse game where all the jocks are idolized and every girl in school shakes her pom-poms.

Ugh. No thank you.

"Fine! Go to work and make coffee all night, but you better text me back!" she ordered, yelling across the parking lot.

I held my hand in the air, waved, and kept on walking to my car. I tossed my bag into the passenger seat of my white

Nissan Maxima and slid behind the wheel. Turning the key, I waited for the engine to kick over so I could get the heck out of here.

Nothing happened. Well, not nothing. It sputtered—a pathetic and miserable sound.

"No. No. No," I said. "Don't do this to me." I tried again and a third time with the same disastrous result. "You stupid hunk of junk."

This was the last thing I needed.

My eyes glanced at the clock on the dash. I was going to be late for work. "Shit," I muttered, my head hitting the back of the seat as my throat closed, tears stinging my eyes. Why today of all days did my car decide to act up? Didn't I have enough to deal with at home? Ever since the night of my eighteenth birthday, my mom had been ill. That had been months ago. The doctors were of little help. They hadn't been able to pinpoint what was wrong, meaning they didn't know how to treat it. As the days went by, I was starting to lose hope they ever would.

I hit the steering wheel, taking out my frustration, anger, and sorrow on the car. "Please start. Please. I promise not to call you names ever again or threaten to drop you off at the junkyard. Cross my heart." I closed my eyes and turned the key.

The engine purred to life.

I exhaled, a slow grin curving my lips, and kissed the steering wheel, not caring who saw me. "I swear I'll wash you this weekend." Yes, I talked to my car. Doesn't everyone?

The drive from school to Sugar and Spice Café was picturesque—a view tourists gawked at but I grew tired of. The mountains were almost always visible in the distance, the air smelled of the sea, and hills and valleys were covered in miles of vineyards that bordered the small town.

I'd been working at the coffee shop after school and during summers since I was a sophomore. It had become an escape, a home away from home. The owner, Naomi, was like a second mom to me and the other high school and college students that worked for her. There were four of us that dedicated our weekends and after-school hours to Naomi Clarke, and she created a fun and safe environment. A fierce, independent, successful businesswoman, Naomi was someone I strived to be—a woman who didn't need to depend on a man. Never married, my boss put everything she had into making the damn best coffee and baked goods in Seaside Heights.

I managed to pull into the employee parking lot with one minute to spare. Talk about cutting it close. If I was anything, I was dependable … and predictable, a punctuation queen. Boring, Jesse and Hannah would say, but boring gave me job security and a bright future. I had plans. Big ones. And this job was going to help me pay for college. Unlike Hannah's parents, who knew the importance of saving money, mine hadn't started a college fund, and any savings they had was spent on Mom's health. I was relying on scholarships and hard-earned cash to get me through veterinarian school.

Grabbing my work clothes from the backseat, I raced across the street and into the alley, a shortcut that led to the back entrance of the café. My hurried footsteps echoed off the buildings lining either side of the empty street. Black garbage bags overflowed out of dumpsters along one wall. I didn't even let my mind think about the critters scurrying about.

A trickle of unease dripped down my spine, and I reached to finger the pendant around my neck. The ancient pearl had been in my mom's family for generations and had been given to me the day I was born. I always wore it, and the weight of it comforted me.

Seaside Heights is a safe place, I repeated to myself, picking up my pace. Just when I thought my day couldn't get any worse, two figures appeared from the shadows, blocking my entrance to the café. My eyes volleyed between them, and I seriously regretted my decision to take the shortcut. I stopped, looked around, and then cursed. Time to get out the pepper spray. Too bad it was lip gloss in my pocket.

A dull ache took up in my gut as I slowed my pace. I guessed they weren't here for the coffee. My legs continued to move forward regardless that my brain screamed to turn and run. Most often your instincts are right.

Both of the figures stood a few feet away and wore suits like the Men in Black with slicked back silvery hair and skin that was a tad too pale, but it was their eyes that chilled my blood. There was something not right about them. Where the color should have been in their irises there was none, just a milky white. Freaky.

I stopped dead in my tracks.

They had to be high. What other explanation was there for the eyes and the unusually white skin?

The taller one angled his head to the side, eyes narrowing. "Karina Lang?" His comrade cracked his knuckles beside him.

Whoa. Didn't see that coming. How did they know my name? My gaze narrowed as I eyed the pair with suspicion, racking my brain. Did I know them? I was positive I didn't. They had faces I wasn't likely ever to forget. The very last thing I expected was for them to know my name. "Depends. Who's asking?" I was shocked my voice didn't shake and that it came out with a lot more bravado than I was feeling.

The taller one smiled as he eyed me, and that smile made

me think of all the horrible situations I'd ever read about a girl alone in an alley. My fear spiked. His gaze dropped to my chest, and I let a startled gasp. My worst nightmare rolled through my head. Were they going to hurt me? Violate me? I was rendered immobile with terror.

His eyes flicked back to mine. He seemed to enjoy the horror he saw on my face. "You have something I want."

"Uh, I think you have me mixed up with someone else. I don't have anything but a work uniform, a granola bar, and my cell phone." I tended to ramble when I was afraid. "And a knife," I added, my hand flying to the back pocket of my jeans, pretending to grab onto an invisible blade.

His buddy's form rippled like liquid, making him go in and out of focus.

I squinted.

Crap on a graham cracker. What were these guys? Aliens?

Either that or I was hallucinating.

He gave a sardonic twist of his lips. "Give us your soul."

So they didn't want my body, just my soul. In that moment, I realized they intended to kill me. How else would they get my soul? I took a step backward. "You guys aren't from around here, are you?"

Neither of them found my sense of humor funny. Their faces remained stoic. Enough of the chitchat. I dropped everything, turned, and ran. Behind me, I heard them both lurch forward and give chase, but I pushed myself harder. I darted to the side around a corner, but I wasn't quick enough. I didn't know what these two guys were or what kind of steroids they were popping, but no human could move that fast.

A beefy arm whisked around my waist. "Gotcha," one of them said with victory in his voice. He grasped a handful of my hair, wrenching my head back against his chest. His grubby fingers fumbled with the front of my shirt. "Let's see what we have here."

Panic flooded me, and like a wild cat, I clawed and scratched anywhere and everywhere I could reach. I didn't care that he still clutched my long dark hair or the agony every moment cost me. I just wanted to break free and save myself from whatever horrible fate they had in store for me. One of my swipes landed across his face, deep enough to draw blood, but not the kind of blood I expected. The cut along his cheek oozed black liquid, bubbling out of the wound like hot tar.

WTF.

My astonishment lasted two whole seconds. He gave a growl that rattled my bones. I'd pissed him off, and my punishment was a backhand across the face, hard enough that it sent me flying. Pain exploded down my face as I hit the ground, shooting through my limbs.

With nowhere else to run, no strength to fight, I curled into a ball against the brick building, huddling into the shadows. Suddenly, I felt something strange. I couldn't explain what happened inside me, maybe I was bleeding internally, but there was tension in my muscles as if they were morphing, stretching, and changing. Tiny needle pricks of heat traveled throughout my body. It wasn't exactly painful, but foreign, a sensation I'd never felt before. But I didn't have time to worry about what bizarre sickness I was coming down with. I had bigger problems.

"Great. She shifted," the one I called Ike said.

What did he mean by *shifted*?

I scurried backward on my hands and feet, except … they weren't hands or feet.

My eyes popped.

What the—

White fur covered my entire body from head to … tail? Holy shit. I had a puffy tail, which might also explain why I stood on all four paws instead of two legs. My long obsidian hair was gone. What had they done to me? Turned me into some kind of animal?

My butt bumped into the wall, and I tried to scream, but all that came out was a low growl that sounded like a warning. My teeth were bared.

Okay, this was going to send me over the edge.

"Easy," Mike said, crouching. "Just give us your powers and we won't hurt you … again," he added.

I tried to tell him I didn't have any powers, but instead a whine came out of my throat.

"Quiet," he hissed, raising his big hand.

I lowered my head, my ears going down as I waited for the impact.

"How about you pick on someone your own size?"

Mike and Ike both froze in response to the deep, unfamiliar, yet very welcomed voice. Lifting my furry chin, I got my first glimpse of my savior.

The mystery man stood well over six feet with hair as dark as the sea at midnight. His expressive brows arched over green eyes that glowed in the dim light. He oozed authority. Power. And sexiness. I wasn't in the position to appreciate his mind-bending attractiveness, but it couldn't be helped. He had the kind of look that demanded to be ogled.

It became clear that neither Mike nor Ike were happy to see the newcomer, giving me a glimmer of hope. Maybe I wouldn't die after all, but truthfully, this new guy was just as much dangerous looking as Mike and Ike were.

His black T-shirt stretched across his broad chest as he lifted both hands in a crisscross over his head, whipping out two blades that had been strapped behind his back. Dayum. He looked about my age, and I was impressed with his apparent skills to wield not one, but two, blades. They looked at home in his hands.

And that was when I noticed the snakes.

I shivered.

Scaly reptiles gave me a mad case of the willies.

The handles on his blades interwove with serpents' tails, extending to coil around his wrists and part of his forearm, making him appear one with the weapons. They hissed with wrath, their heads near the middle of his arm. I'd never seen anything like them. One second they'd been ornaments on the handles, and the next, they were living, breathing vipers.

"This doesn't concern you, Sin Eater," spat one of the odd men, glaring at the mystery man like he was something he scraped off the bottom of his overpriced shit-kickers.

He moved into the alley. "That's where you're wrong. It's my job to protect her."

Protect me?

I snuck farther into the corner, my tail tucked against the wall. *Tail.* God, I had a tail! And as I looked to the new guy, I realized I was a whole lot smaller—about the size of a medium dog.

"You think you can take both of us?" the two chuckled, their cockiness showing in their disregard of the one they called "Sin Eater."

A whisper of a smirk pulled at his lips. "Without breaking a sweat. Now, can we get this over with? You're interrupting my job."

The lanky man's fingers curled into fists. Things were about to blow south, and I needed to make sure I didn't get swept away. But at the first slash of the Sin Eater's sword, I found my paws wouldn't move. Really, where could I go as a … what was I?

One of them made a low snarl deep in his throat, an animal-like sound. Together, the two idiots lunged toward the stranger. A second before they reached him, the mysterious guy spun, letting his blades whiz through the air. There was a hiss like a thousand snakes at once, and then one of the blades sliced through the abdomen of the one who was slightly smaller.

As if things could have gotten any weirder, once the blade cleared his flesh, his milky eyes went wide. His mouth dropped open in a silent scream, and then the bastard exploded in a dark cloud of smoke that hovered in the air like thick smog. The head of the snake from the blade that pierced him reared up off the mysterious man's forearm and opened its mouth. A forked tongue shot out, siphoning the dark smoke from the air until there was nothing left of Ike.

"Enjoy the trip back to the otherworld." The strange man pointed his other sword at the other—the one that dripped black gunk. "Your turn."

His eyes bounced between the sword and the stranger's face. He must not have liked his chances. The coward turned and ran.

The Sin Eater's lips curved. "Oh good, a runner."

He didn't get more than a few steps. Like a whip, the Sin Eater lashed one of the snakes out at the attacker's feet. It coiled, tripping him up so he kissed the ground. Black blood dripped from his nose, but he wasn't about to give up his chance at escape. He scrambled to get back on his feet, but the swordsman was at his side and tossed him across the alley. His body slammed into the brick wall before crumbling to the ground. The impact should have knocked him out, but not this dude.

"Is that the best you can do?" The attacker didn't seem to be in a position to talk smack in my opinion.

"Please. I'm just getting started, Silvermyst." The dark-haired guy flicked his wrists, spinning the sword in his left hand. With no hesitation in his movements, the Sin Eater slammed the tip of a blade into the gut of the Silvermyst, as he had called him.

The Silvermyst met the same fate as his partner—the other snake taking a turn at gulping up his hovering ashes.

I had definitely stumbled into the Twilight Zone or an alternate universe. This kind of shit didn't happen in Seaside Heights, Washington. We had our share of weirdos, but this took it to a whole new level of strange.

I was going to puke.

The assassin sheathed both of his weapons behind his back and came to crouch in front of me. I stared into his green eyes. His thick lashes circled them, and I felt myself drowning in the depths of color. Wariness fluttered in my belly. What was he planning to do? Would he kill me next? Or was it possible he would know how to help me?

"My name is Devyn St. Cyr, and I won't hurt you. I'm here to help, Kitten." He laid a hand on my furry head, and I let out a whimper.

Kitten? Was that what I had turned into? A little kitten? But that didn't seem right. I was definitely bigger than a cat.

If he tried to pick me up, I'd probably bite him. I wasn't going anywhere with anyone, especially with a guy who played with swords and snakes. But it didn't matter what I wanted, because something started to happen under his touch. The tingles I felt earlier came back, spreading from my head throughout my furry body, building and building in intensity until it became too much. I'd had enough. The whole situation overwhelmed me. My eyes lost focus, blurring Devyn's face, and my head sunk, suddenly feeling like it was full of cotton.

And then it was night-night for Karina, and I knew nothing but darkness.

Check out book one on Amazon!
Click here to get your next shifter fix.

ABOUT THE AUTHOR

USA TODAY Bestselling author J.L. Weil lives in Illinois where she writes Teen & New Adult Paranormal Romances about spunky, smart mouth girls who always wind up in dire situations. For every sassy girl, there is an equally mouthwatering, overprotective guy. Of course, there is lots of kissing. And stuff

An admitted addict to Love Pink clothes, raspberry mochas from Starbucks, and Jensen Ackles. She loves gushing about books and Supernatural with her readers.

She is the author of the International Bestselling Raven & Divisa series.

Stalk Me Online
www.jlweil.com
jenniferlweil@gmail.com

CPSIA information can be obtained
at www.ICGtesting.com
Printed in the USA
BVHW031138170219
540465BV00001B/52/P

9 781985 371552